HEART-SHAPED COOKIES

Bilingual Press/Editorial Bilingüe

Address

Bilingual Press
Hispanic Research Center
Arizona State University
PO Box 875303
Tempe, Arizona 85287-5303
(480) 965-3867

Heart-Shaped Cookies

AND OTHER STORIES

David Rice

Bilingual Press/Editorial Bilingüe
TEMPE, ARIZONA

Library of Congress Cataloging-in-Publication Data

Rice, David, 1964-
Heart-shaped cookies / David Rice.
p. cm.
Summary: A collection of ten short stories reprinted from "Give the pig a chance" and other anthologies, nine new stories, and a play by Mike D. Garcia based on Rice's short story, "She flies."
ISBN 978-1-931010-79-5 (softcover : alk. paper)
1. Mexican Americans—Juvenile fiction. 2. Texas—Juvenile fiction. 3. Children's stories, American. [1. Mexican Americans—Fiction. 2. Texas—Fiction. 3. Short stories.] I. Garcia, Mike D. She flies. II. Title.
PZ7.R36184He 2011
[Fic]—dc22

2011007946

PRINTED IN THE UNITED STATES OF AMERICA

Front cover images: *David Rice (photo), 123RF.com (cookie cutter)*
Cover and interior design by John Wincek

Permissions and Acknowledgments

"The Crash Room." First published in *Working Days: Short Stories about Teenagers at Work*, 1997. Reprinted by permission of Persea Books, Inc.

"Tomboy Forgiveness." First published in *Baseball Crazy: Ten Short Stories That Cover All the Bases*, 2009. Reprinted by permission of the author.

"Tied to Zelda." First published in *Tripping over the Lunch Lady and Other School Stories*, 2004. Reprinted by permission of Puffin Books, an imprint of Penguin Group.

The front cover photo is of Don José Correa Dávila, owner of La Mexicana *panadería* in Elsa, Texas. Photo taken in 1998 by David Rice.

The writer expresses his appreciation to Dr. Jaime Mejia, Dr. Martha L. Brunson, and Beverly Braud of the English Department of Texas State University. Also, to my dad and mom, my sister Renée and my brother Roger, Josh Dubose, and friends: Laura V. Rodríguez, Francisco and Yvonne Guajardo, Daniel, Andrea, Mac, Yvette Benavides, Harry Mazer, Patricia Fraga, Samantha Smith, Christopher Caselli, Linda St. George, Nancy Mercado, Carol Wilson, Natasha Sinutko Morgan, and Julie Hudgens.

This book is dedicated to my grandparents and tías, Lucía, Minnie, and Carmen; to Eduardo and Eloisa Cuellar; and to David Hume Rice.

Contents

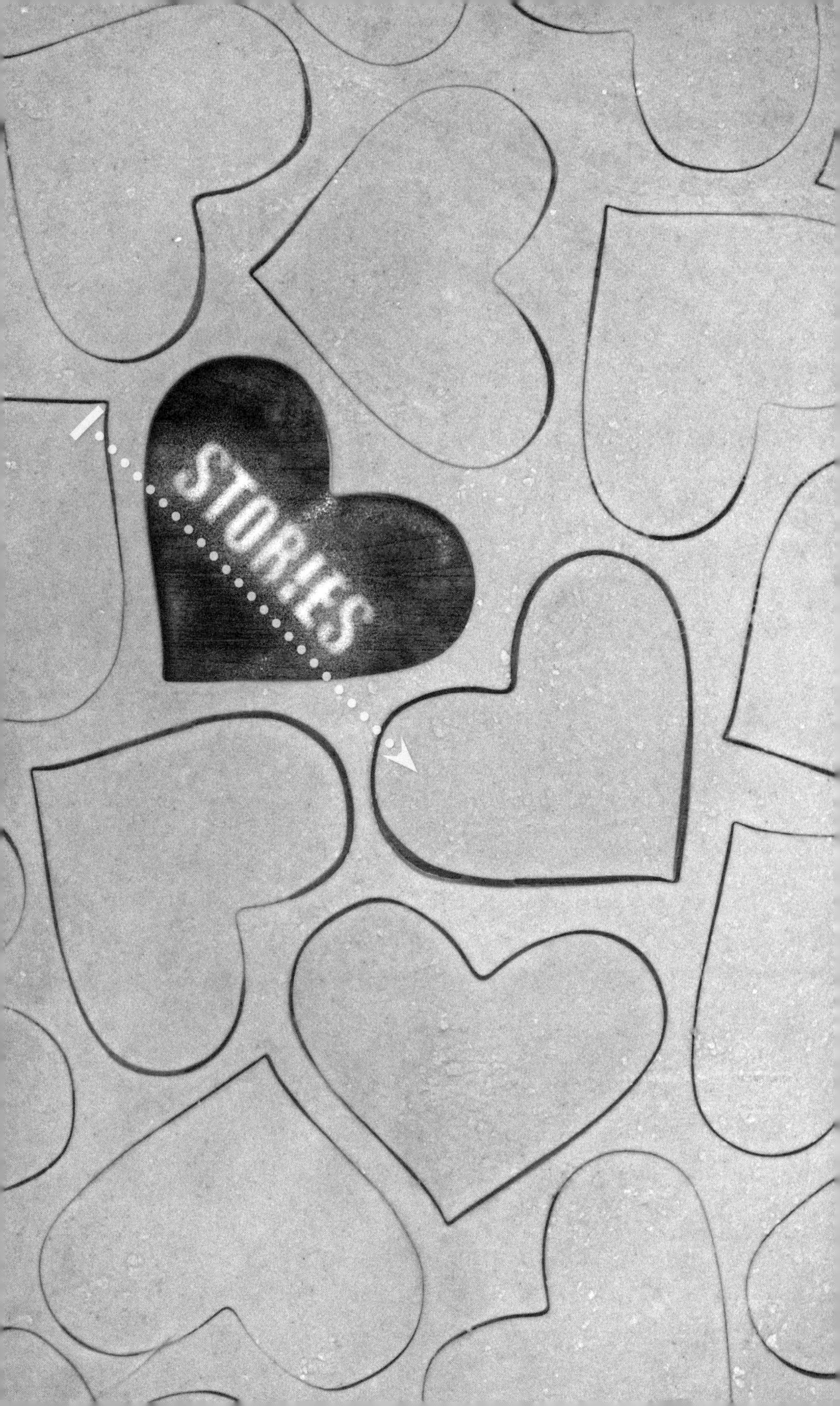
STORIES

Tied to Zelda

My next-door neighbor, Zelda Fuerte, scares me and gives me the chills at the same time. She is the biggest tomboy in town and the evil twin sister I never wanted. She can outrun any boy, climb a tree faster than a cat, and spit the farthest. My dad always invites her to our house to play since she doesn't have a father around. She's the son my father wanted me to be. He always says, "Do it like Zelda." When my dad isn't around, Zelda likes to play "Tie Up," a game she invented. She is always tying me up, but I always escape.

The only time I am safe is summer. That's when Zelda, her mother, and sisters drive to Utah to pick fruit. My father and I help Zelda and her family board up their house and load their van. Zelda always looks a little sad when she leaves, and I am too, since I have to mow their lawn while they are away. In the fall, I only see Zelda in the school halls and we exchange a semi-friendly "Hi." Other than that, I stay far away from her.

Our school has a yearly tradition called Sadie Hawkins Day, a day when boys and girls are paired up to compete in a three-legged race and an egg-tossing contest. I think it sounds kinda dumb, but there are big prizes worth big bucks. If you win the three-legged race, you get two passes to Splash World for the whole summer and free hot dogs. That's pretty cool. If you win the egg-tossing contest, you get two passes to sports camp at the local college. Three weeks of running and sweating and the whole time coaches yelling? No thanks.

Anyway, one week before Sadie Hawkins Day, the teachers got all the fifth-graders into the cafeteria and they brought out two big baskets, one with the boys' names and the other with the girls' names. Our drama teacher spun the baskets around a few times and took a name from each basket. He was really hamming it up. "Now hear this, now hear this," he said over a megaphone. Then he called a girl's name real slowly, and there was an "Oooooooooo" throughout the cafeteria. Then he called out the boy's name, and everyone cheered, whistled, and clapped for each team. The next girl's name he pulled out was "Zeeellllda Fuerte!" That's how he called everyone's name. When her name was called out, my best friend Jorge leaned over to me.

"Man, whoever is Zelda's partner will win both contests," he said.

"*Ffft*, forget it. I don't want to go to sports camp," I said.

"Don't you want the Splash World pass?" Jorge asked. "Free admission for the whole summer and free hot dogs too."

"Yeah, it'd be cool, but I don't want to be tied up to Zelda," I said.

"What's wrong with being tied up to Zelda?" Jorge asked.

"She's a knot nazi," I said.

Our teacher pulled out a boy's name and held it high. He smiled and pointed at me like he was a game show host. "Allllfoooooonsoooo Flores!"

Jorge and the whole cafeteria started laughing. I looked over at Zelda and she threw her arms up as if she had just lost the national championship. After all the names were called, Zelda walked up to me.

"Alfonso, after school, meet me in the gym," she said.

"But I have a computer club meeting and I'm—" I tried to finish, but she cut me off.

"After school in the gym. Don't make me come looking for you. I know where you live." She spun around and walked off in a huff.

After school, during the computer club meeting, Jorge asked me if he could borrow my Splash World pass.

"Look, I don't want to be tied up, and I don't want to throw eggs," I said.

"C'mon, don't be a baby. It's just your ankles tied together and everybody likes throwing eggs," Jorge said. "And if you win, we can share Splash World and hot dogs."

"Well, if you want the passes so bad, why don't you and your partner practice, and you can win the passes to Splash World."

"Because Zelda's the best. No one can beat her," Jorge said.

Then the door busted open. And there was Zelda looking really mad. My first thought was to run, but she was blocking the only escape route.

"I told you to be in the gym after school so we could practice!" she shouted firmly.

"Can't you find someone else?" I squeaked.

"I can't; you know the rules. Monday we'll practice. We're going to win," she said, and slammed the door.

Jorge threw his arms up like he had won a gold medal. "Splash World, here we come!"

I was a little worried, but the weekend was here, and I thought Zelda would forget, but she didn't. On Sunday night she came to my house, and my mom let her in. I was helping my father tighten a nut under the bathroom sink, unaware that Zelda was working on my mother. My dad told me to get him a glass of water, and when I walked into the kitchen, they were sitting at the breakfast table, and Mom looked thrilled. She waved a friendly dishrag at me.

"You didn't tell me you and Zelda were partners in the Sadie Hawkins Day festival."

"But I don't—" I managed to say, then Zelda cut me off.

"If we win the three-legged race, we get two passes to Splash World, and if we win the egg-tossing contest, we get two passes to summer sports camp. Isn't that great?" Zelda said, all happy.

My mother shook her excited dishrag. "Wow, when is the festival? I mean, you two need to practice."

It was exactly what Zelda wanted to hear. "That's why I came by," she said. "The festival is this Friday, and we need to practice every day after school."

"*Ffft*, forget it," I said. "I don't want to go to sports camp."

My mother turned to me, narrowed her eyes, and shook her now-angry dishrag. "Whatever. You're going to be partners with Zelda."

Zelda smirked at me, and when my mother turned back to her, she looked all hurt and sad. Zelda sighed. "Well, Mrs. Flores, if Alfonso doesn't want to be my partner, I guess I'll have to find someone else." And she lowered her head.

My mother tossed the emotionally wrecked dishrag on the table. Then my father walked in with a wrench in his hand and put it down on the table with a hard metal sound. "What do you mean you don't want to be Zelda's partner?"

"But, Dad, I don't want to go to sports camp," I said.

He picked up his wrench and waved it like a warlock ready to cast a spell. "Alfonso, you're going to practice every day with Zelda. All you do is play on your computer. And if you don't practice, you'll find your computer in the trash can," Dad said, and tossed his wrench on the kitchen table.

Zelda threw her arms up in glee. "Great. Every day we'll practice till we get it right."

My mother smiled and picked up the happy dishrag and waved it. "Practice makes perfect."

I dropped my head in defeat.

In the morning I cautiously walked the school halls. Turning corners slowly, trying to avoid Zelda. Then I saw her marching toward me. She yelled, "Freeze!" I took a step back and saw the boys' restroom and thought about running in there, but when I turned, there was Monica, Zelda's best friend. I took another step back and felt a heavy hand on my shoulder. I turned around, and there stood Zelda.

"Where do you think you're going?" Zelda asked.

"I have to pee really bad," I said.

Zelda pushed me against the lockers. "Squeeze your legs and hold it," she said.

Then Zelda poked my chest with each word as she said, "Today after school. You better be there." Monica poked my chest too. "You better. We want the sports passes," she said.

I was scared, but when I saw Jorge coming down the hall I shouted, "Help me!" I felt better when Jorge walked up, but then he and Zelda acted like they were best friends.

"What's up?" Jorge said to Zelda.

"Just making sure Alfonso meets me after school."

"He'll be there. We want the passes to Splash World," Jorge said as he crossed his arms.

"But I don't want to play Tie Up," I pleaded.

Jorge looked confused. "Tie Up?" he said.

Zelda poked my chest. "You better play Tie Up, or else." She paused and grinned. "I'll tell your father, and he'll take away your computer."

I looked at Jorge for help. "Quit acting like a baby," he said. "Everybody likes being tied up and throwing eggs."

After school Zelda escorted me outside to the recess area. She put down her backpack and took out a piece of rope. "I always carry my own rope," she said as she raised her eyebrows a couple of times. Fear swelled in my stomach. Zelda tied my ankle to hers real tight and I felt my bones crushing. She said we had to run like one person. We started running, but I tripped and made us fall. She shook her head and pulled me up. I thought for sure she was going to beat me up, but instead she smiled.

"You OK?" she asked.

I nodded as I brushed off my jeans.

Monica and two other girls cheered us on.

"C'mon, Alfonso, you can do it!"

They shouted like cheerleaders. I never had anyone cheer for me, and it felt good. Zelda put her arm around my waist, and I put my arm around her shoulders. She said to hold her tight.

"OK," she said. "We start off slow until we're together, and then we speed it up."

We took small slow steps and then faster, bigger ones, and then we were running. Zelda's friends were cheering louder, and I felt like a sports star. We slowed down to a stop, and turned around and started all over again. We ran back and forth, and each time we were getting faster and faster. Then we fell again, but this time we fell hard. I banged my head against the ground and got a nasty red mark, but no blood. Zelda and her friends helped me up. They had their hands all over me, brushing off the dry grass and fixing my hair, asking me if I was OK and stuff like that. Then Zelda brought out a golf ball.

"Time to practice egg tossing." She raised the white ball to my eyes. "Use both hands and keep your eyes on the ball."

We started at five feet from each other and tossed the ball back and forth. Each time I dropped the ball, we started all over again, and she'd say, "Only the ball," but it was hard for me to see the white blurry object. She'd toss the ball, and I'd lose it in the clouds. Maybe I needed glasses. Each time I dropped the ball, I thought Zelda was going to get mad, but she didn't.

"This is practice. You can mess up all you want, but not on game day," she said.

I nodded. "Right, Coach," I said.

She smiled and punched my arm.

I found out that other teams were practicing—even Jorge was practicing with his partner, and that got me pumped. It made me want to win the race and the contest. Zelda and I could run the three-legged race really fast, and I was getting better at catching the ball. The second it touched my fingers, I closed my hands tightly around it. I could tell Zelda was proud of me.

The night before the festival, Zelda came over to my house with a bag of pan dulce.

"What's this?" I asked.

"I got you some heart-shaped cookies and marranitos. I think people should be rewarded for their hard work."

She smiled and put the bag out, and I was about to take it. Then I noticed she was looking around me and she whispered in a sneaky tone, "Who's here?"

"Nobody, my parents—"

She cut me off and snatched the bag away and began poking me in the chest with her stiff finger and raised her voice. "Tomorrow I want to win." Her face was inches from mine.

I backed up. "Hey, I'll do my best."

"You better. If you don't, I'm tying you up to a tree in the middle of nowhere and let the ants eat you."

"Look, what's the big deal? It's just a stupid contest," I said, shrugging my shoulders.

"I want the passes to sports camp," she said in deep voice, and lowered her head like a charging bull.

"But who wants to spend three weeks at a sports camp?" I said.

"I do," she said. "I'd rather be at a sports camp than in Utah with my jerk father."

I knew her parents were separated, but I thought her father lived in a nearby town.

"I thought your father lived in the Valley."

Zelda shook her head and let out a deep sigh. "No, he lives in Utah, and we have to stay with him and my tío. They're both jerks. All they do is drink beer and smoke all night."

"Can't you stay somewhere else?"

"No, think we're rich or something? I want me and my mom and sisters to stay here for the summer. If I get the sports passes, my mom said we'd stay and she'd find a job here."

"Well, if we win the three-legged race, can't you trade your Splash World pass with someone for the sports camp pass?" I asked.

"No, I promised my mother I'd let my little sisters have the Splash World pass if I won it." Her eyes got all watery. "Don't you see? We have to win the egg toss. I don't want my mother to be around my father."

She dropped her head and let out a sad sigh. She held out the bag of pan dulce, and I took it.

She sniffed a little and looked up at me. "Just do your best, OK?"

I nodded. "I promise," I said.

The next day when I walked to the recess area, there was lots going on. The high school conjunto band was playing, and there was a popcorn machine, chili frito pies, fajita tacos, buttered elotes, and raspas in all flavors. The sports camp had a banner up, and so did Splash World. There were kids tied at the ankles walking around and others on the ground all tangled up. I felt a tap on my shoulder and turned around, and there was Zelda. She didn't waste any time. She gave me a high five and tied our ankles together, and we walked around the recess area like one big person.

There was a long line of three-legged kids for the three-legged race, but Zelda said to focus on the finish line, not the competition. I was a little jumpy when we got in our starting positions, but Zelda put her arm around me, and we held each other tight. I heard the whistle blow, and we were flying. I could hear our hearts pounding when we crossed the finish line, but we couldn't stop. We tripped all over the place and hit the ground rolling.

But it was worth it because we won first place. Zelda and I were on the ground laughing through our bruises, and Jorge came running over to us.

"Splash World, oh yeah," he said.

Zelda and I walked around trying to shake off our scraped elbows and knees. Kids I didn't know were walking up to us saying what a great job we had done.

The egg toss had even more kids than the three-legged race. The teachers placed a long white string across the ground to divide the teams. Zelda put her hand up to give another high five. Two teachers walked between the teams carrying cartons of twenty-four eggs. When the teachers walked up to us, they asked who was going to choose the egg. I pointed to Zelda.

Zelda took one egg and held it with her fingers. She moved her wrist back and forth, studying the egg, looking for little thin cracks. She put it back and took another one. The teachers were like: "We don't have all day." Zelda held that egg and studied it too and let the weight of it move her arm up and down. She raised it up to my eye level. "Only the ball," she said.

The rules were easy. The kids on the right of our drama teacher threw first. Each time you caught the egg, you'd take one step back. Getting farther and farther apart. The last team left without breaking their egg won the contest.

When the whistle blew, all the kids threw their eggs except Zelda. She waited, and I could hear kids dropping their eggs and lots of laughing. I turned to look, but Zelda shouted, "Hey, focus on me and the egg."

I nodded. She tossed her egg with a nice gentle arch, and I put my hands together and caught it easily, but we were only five feet from each other. We took another step back and the whistle blew. Zelda put her hands up and gestured for me to wait until the other kids threw theirs. Through my side vision I could see eggs all over the sky, I heard eggs breaking and kids screaming, "Ahhhhhhhhh" and "Yuck," but Zelda kept gesturing for me to look at her.

After a few seconds she nodded, and I tossed my egg. She caught it like it belonged to her. Toss after toss I could hear more eggs breaking and the crowd laughing, but I kept my eyes on Zelda. Finally we were really far from each other, and there were only three teams left.

Then the teachers brought us closer and made us put our arms out so we could touch fingertips with the kids on each side.

The whistle blew, but none of the kids threw their eggs. I looked to the right of Zelda, and there was Jorge waving.

Our drama teacher shouted through his megaphone, "Welllllll, somebody throw an egg."

We didn't say anything for a moment and then Zelda spoke up.

"We'll throw first," she said. The crowd went, "Oooooooooo." I looked at Zelda, and she walked up to me.

"Do your best." She handed me the egg. Then she ran back to her position and nodded at me. I took a few deep breaths and threw the egg with all my strength. The egg had a high arch. I overthrew it. Zelda had to take several quick steps back and dove for the egg. I put my hands to my face ready to scream, but Zelda was a super athlete. The egg disappeared into her body, and she rolled on the ground and jumped up with the egg safe in her hand. The crowd went wild.

The next team threw their egg, but the boy threw way too short. The girl ran forward fast and caught it, but the egg exploded in her hands and face. The crowd went, "Eeeeeelooooooooooo," and there was tons of laughter. After the crowd settled down, Jorge threw his egg, and it was perfect. His partner didn't have to move an inch, and it floated right into her hands. The crowd cheered and clapped like a bunch of excited monkeys.

Our drama teacher put his hand up. "OK, now both teams must throw at the same time."

The crowd went wild again.

We all took a step back, and Zelda was so far away, she was a blur. I looked at Jorge and back at Zelda, and I put my hands up in a time-out gesture like they do in sports games. "Time out," I shouted.

I heard the crowd yelling, "Hey, you can't do that! Hurry up, throw it!"

I ran to the middle of the field and gestured for Jorge to meet me. He ran to me.

"What's up?" he said.

"Listen, I don't think I can catch the egg. I can't see anything," I said. "Let's make a deal. If you catch the egg, you give me your pass to sports camp, and I'll give you my pass to Splash World."

I could tell he wasn't going for it, so I added more. "And I'll loan you any video game I have for a whole month."

Jorge rolled his eyes. "*Ffft*, only one?"

"OK, two," I said.

Jorge put his hand on his chin and lightly stroked it. "Yeah, but what if you do catch the egg?"

"Then I'll give you my pass to Splash World and my pass to sports camp."

"And the video games?" Jorge grinned.

"Yes, yes. You can still borrow them."

Jorge put out his hand and we shook on it. "It's a deal," he said.

I ran back to my position and rubbed my sweaty palms on my shirt and nodded.

Zelda took a step back and threw the egg like a football. It was a prefect spiral. But it was going too fast. I had to step back and just as it touched my hands, I tripped over my feet. The egg went through my hands and hit me squarely on the forehead. There was egg all over me, and I wiped my face and looked at Jorge, who was laughing like a nut with an egg in his hands, jumping up and down, like a freaked out kangaroo. "Splash World and hot dogs!" he kept shouting.

He jumped over to Zelda, and I could tell he was telling her the deal I made with him, and she began jumping up and down and ran toward me. She gave me a high five and punched my arm. She put her arm around my shoulders, and I put my arm around hers, and we walked without being tied together.

That night my parents came to my room and knocked on the door frame.

"Hey, mijo, Zelda's mother just called and told us what you did today. Your mother and I are very proud of you," Dad said.

"Thanks," I said.

"Listen, tomorrow we're going to buy you a summer pass for Splash World. Sound good to you?"

I thought for a moment. "Thanks, Dad, thanks, Mom, but I'd rather go to sports camp."

They looked a little confused. "But we thought you wanted to go to Splash World," Mom said.

"Well, yeah, but Zelda is going to sports camp, and she might need a partner," I said.

Tomboy Forgiveness

"Get ready, 'cause this is gonna knock you over," Tía Berta said with a sly grin as she leaned over the pitching mound with the eager softball in her hand. Our mother, standing firm over home plate, swirled her bat and spit. "You can't strike me out," she said. When my sister, Rosana, and I saw Mom spit, we knew she was going to hit the ball with all her strength, so we backed up. Berta adjusted her baseball cap, kicked some dirt off the pitching mound, and spun her arm in a blur, and the ball shot out like a cannonball. In one quick move Mom pulled and swung the bat at full speed and slammed the ball in our direction. "I got it," Rosana shouted, and the ball smacked her glove. She raised the ball in the air. "It's still hot." Mom adjusted her cap. "Think I'm ready for the tournament this weekend?" she said with a wide smile. Berta let out a booming laugh and kicked dirt off the pitching mound like a bull ready to charge. "Girl, you and me. In the final," she said.

Berta was our mom's best friend, even though they played softball against each other with every fiber of their being. We called Berta "Tía Berta" because we saw her so much, and she was also our mother's hairdresser and made sure our mom was the only Mexican American woman in town with bright blond hair or cherry red hair. Every three months Mom walked into the house with a new color and a new attitude. "Keep them guessing," she'd say, and she was the same way in softball.

You never knew what she was going to do. Line drive, bunt, grounder, or hit a home run. But you weren't going to be ready. Our father said the same about her. "Esta mujer," he'd say in frustration, but every year his brake shop sponsored Mom's softball team with new uniforms and equipment. The only catch was, he liked to be third base coach, and he was good at yelling and swinging his arms like a deranged monkey. At every game he'd shout orders like a bully. The softball team lasted longer than their marriage.

When we were little, Mom and Dad were always fighting, and then all of a sudden he found a new wife and a new family. We knew the brand-new sons because they were our age and we saw them at school all the time. It was something we got used to, and by the time we got to junior high, everybody knew the story, so it didn't bother us too much. When our parents divorced it was Berta who was by our mother's side through the whole ordeal, and she did her best to cheer Mom up.

Our hometown of Edcouch hosted the softball tournament, and teams from Elsa, La Villa, Monte Alto, La Blanca, Hargill, Santa Rosa, and Weslaco filled up our ballpark. Edcouch only had 2,656 people, but during the tournament our town doubled in size.

Every year Mom and Tía Berta were the rock stars of the tournament, and people shook their hands as they walked by. Mom was best hitter in the league, and Tía Berta, the best pitcher. When Beto's Brake Shop played against Berta's Beauty Shop, the bleachers would get packed with fans cheering for both teams. There were no losers.

One week before the tournament, the Rubén pony express broke down and Rosana got some messed-up news. Rosana was in eighth grade and had a class with Rubén, our dad's stepson. They got along OK, and Mom used Rubén as a post office. If Mom wanted to send a message to Dad, she'd write it down on a piece of paper and seal it in an envelope and give it to Rosana, and Rosana would give it to Rubén, and Rubén gave it to Dad. It wasn't very mature, but the postage was free.

I was walking down the school halls between classes when Rosana came barreling toward me, brushing kids aside like a hurricane with the latest news. She took my arm and pushed me against the wall.

"Guess what Rubén just told me?" she said, like it was the most important thing she ever heard.

I jerked my arm from her grasp. "What, that he wets the bed?"

"*Pffff*. Grosero." Then in a secret hush, she said, "He told me that Dad is seeing some other woman."

"What?" I said.

"Yeah, Rubén said that his mom kicked Dad out of the house," Rosana said.

"Ah, man, are you serious?" I said with a chuckle, 'cause I thought it was kinda funny.

"Yeah, and you'll never guess who Dad is seeing."

I shrugged my shoulders. "Who?"

Rosana took a deep breath and shook her head in disbelief. "Tía Berta."

You know how in cartoons when someone gets hit on the head with a frying pan and their head vibrates, making ringing sounds? That's what I felt like when my sister told me that Dad was seeing Tía Berta.

"What?" I grabbed my sister's arms to keep my head from shaking to pieces.

"I know, I know. It's so messed up," she said.

"Does Mom know?" I said.

"I don't know."

"What are we going to do?" I said.

My sister let out a sigh. "Poor Mom," she said.

The rest of the day I walked in a daze, turning over the possibilities of Mom's reaction. Even though my parents were divorced and all, it was still uncool what Tía Berta was doing, but at the same time it wasn't any of my business. That afternoon my sister and I walked home together, something we didn't often do, but we needed each other. It was Monday night softball practice, and we thought that probably one of Mom's teammates would tell her the news. When we got home we decided to clean up the house real nice so if Mom came home in a bad mood, at least the house was clean. By 5:30 Mom wasn't home yet, and we called her cell phone, but she didn't answer.

"Do you think Mom knows?" I asked my sister.

Rosana threw her arms up. "By now the whole town knows," she said.

It was close to 10:00 when Mom walked in the house. We were watching TV and we stood up. She was wearing her softball practice clothes and was covered in sweat. I don't remember my parents' divorce, but what I was feeling must have been what I felt when our father left us. Mom wears her emotions like a jacket. Everyone can see what she's thinking.

"Mom, you OK?" my sister asked.

"You guys heard, huh?"

We nodded.

"I ran four miles after practice. You know how it is. You just gotta sweat it out." She pulled her head back and exhaled. Then she brought her head down and shook it like boxers do before a fight. "I'm just going to stay focused on the tournament."

The next day a few of her teammates came to the house to go over the batting order. Mom's softball friends were loud and loved to drink beer out of bottles as they decided who would hit singles, doubles, and home runs. Tía Berta was usually there to help out with the list since she knew the batting styles of every player, but not this time. Her name wasn't even mentioned, and her laugh didn't fill our house. All week long there was this dark cloud hanging over Mom. I had never seen her look so sad, and I knew that the tournament was going to be make or break for her.

Saturday morning was gloomy, and there were low dark clouds as far as you could see. Mom had her game face on, and so did my sister. Rosana was the bat girl and equipment manager, and took her jobs seriously. My job was to mix Gatorade in a big cooler with lots of ice and stay out of their way as we loaded Mom's truck. I rode in the back of the truck surrounded by mesh nylon bags of gear for the short drive to the City of Edcouch Ball Park. Four fields of hard-hitting softball action. The tournament was fast. Only eight teams with four fields and double elimination, and each game with a time limit of one hour and fifteen minutes.

When we parked, Mom's teammates walked up with the game schedule. The first team they would play was Berta's Beauty Shop. Mom nodded. "Well then, they will be the first team to lose." When both teams stood in line on the field for the "Star Spangled Banner," you could feel the frustration between the teams. It was strange because the players were all friends and many of them had grown up together, but they didn't know how to act. Fans were at a loss too, but secretly they were taking sides. But in the end, everyone knew the game would have the answers.

Our father stayed away from Mom, and Berta stayed away from our father. My sister and I said very little, and cheering for Beto's Brake Shop didn't feel right because we felt like we were cheering for our father, since his name was on their uniforms. The game started off with Berta pitching the first strikeout of the day. You could see Berta taking the game seriously and doing her best, but she couldn't strike Mom out.

Each time Mom was up to bat, she got on base. With four minutes left in the game, Berta's Beauty Shop was up by one. Our father made short paces behind third base, clapping his hands. "Come on, the clock is ticking." Mom's team had one runner on second, and our mother was up to bat. Mom picked up some dirt and rubbed her hands. Berta adjusted her cap and put the ball right down the middle. "Strike one," the umpire shouted. Mom took a step back and moved her head side to side and then returned to the batter's box with the bat pulled back tight. Berta pitched a blur, and the umpire shouted, "Strike two." Mom took a step back and gave her bat a couple of short swings and then got ready for Berta's third pitch. Berta threw low, but this time Mom's bat was there to say hello and goodbye.

The ball sailed deep into right field, and the woman on second scrambled home. Mom sprinted through first and rounded second before the outfielder threw the ball in. Our father was shouting, "Go, go, go! Take it home!" My sister and I were standing, shouting the same thing along with the crowd. Mom blew through third, and Berta caught the ball and threw it hard to home. As the ball touched the catcher's glove, Mom slammed her, and the ball shot out of the glove. "Safe!" the umpire shouted, with one minute left on the clock as Mom and the catcher hit the ground. There was a roar of cheers from the stands. Berta's Beauty Shop advanced to the loser's bracket, and Beto's Brake Shop advanced to the winner's bracket.

By noon, my sister and I had sore throats from all the yelling and shouting. Mom's team couldn't make a mistake if they tried. Meanwhile, Berta's team was on a winning streak in the loser's bracket. Talk throughout the tournament was about a final game between Beto's Brake Shop and Berta's Beauty Shop, and each game moved Mom and Berta closer. Mom's team cut Juanita's Flower Shop to pieces, and Berta's team burned down the Hot Tamale House. Usually the teams who lost would leave, but everyone knew that the final game was more than just a game, and lots of people got on their cell phones, and even more people showed up.

My sister told me that people were betting to see who would win the tournament, and some were even betting that our mom and Tía Berta would get into a fistfight.

"What?" I said.

"You know that Mom and Tía Berta were big tomboys," my sister said with a worried look. "We need to talk to Mom."

Five minutes before the final game, we told Mom about the bets going around.

Mom smacked her fist into her glove. "I'll bet your father started those stupid bets."

"But Mom, you're not going to get into a fight with Tía Berta, are you?" my sister asked.

Mom looked shocked. "Berta is my best friend. I would never hurt her."

"But you're not talking to her. And all your friends are mad at her," I said.

"But I'm not mad at her," Mom said. "I'm just hurt." She could see we were worried. "Hey, it's going to be OK. I'm not going to let your father ruin this too. Just cheer for Berta like you cheer for me, and everything will be fine." We gave each other a group hug, and Mom darted to her team.

In the stands, fans were stacked like human watermelons, and people were standing all over the place in the 100-degree heat, but it was worth it. Within thirty minutes of play, Berta's team was up by two, and my mom's team was struggling to get a grip on the game. One hour into the final, Mom and Berta squared off again, but Berta was too hot to stop, and in three fast pitches, Mom was out. When Berta's team was up to bat, Mom's team didn't let one player past first base.

There were only seven minutes left in the game when Mom's team came up to bat. They were down by two, but you could feel something was going to happen. The first batter, Virna, knocked the first pitch into left field, and made it to first base. The second batter, our mom, walked to home plate with a wall of cheers behind her. Berta stayed focused and burned the first pitch. Strike! Mom stepped back and regained her thoughts and raised her bat for the second pitch. Berta's second pitch was faster. "Strike two!" the umpire shouted. The fans went nuts with whistles and shouts.

Mom stepped back from the plate, adjusted her cap, got in the batter's box, and pointed to left field. The crowd let out an

"Oooooooo." Berta took in a deep breath and fired another rocket, but this time Mom exploded the ball as promised. The crowd went crazy. Mom reached second base, and Virna advanced to third base. You could see our father already giving orders to Virna about getting home.

Two minutes were left in the game, and the third batter, Delia, was always worth a hit. Berta tightened up and then threw like lightning, but Delia's bat was already in motion, and in a flash the ball went right back at Berta. The crowd let out a gasp as the ball hit Berta right in the face. Berta let out a loud cry, and the way she went down, you could tell she was hurt. Our father started shouting at Virna to run, and Virna made it home. Our Mom ran through third and then slowed down and looked back at Berta and then ran to Berta. Our father went nuts, shouting, "What are you doing? Forget her!"

Mom knelt by Berta and helped her sit up, but our father kept shouting. The crowd fell silent, and all you could hear was our father screaming insults at our mother. Mom looked at our father, who was stomping and kicking dirt like a spoiled kid. Then she looked at us. We were in the dugout, and both of us were clutching the steel fence. My sister's eyes began to water, and she turned to me and took my hand, and we nodded at Mom. We could see tears rolling down Mom's face, and she smiled at us. She slowly reached for the ball, and our father went ape crazy and starting screaming, "Don't you dare touch that ball! Leave it alone."

Our Mom put her hand on the ball, clenched it, and picked it up. She raised it above her head for the world to see, and everyone held their breath. Then there was a break in the dark clouds and a ray of light embraced Tía Berta and Mom. Mom then turned her hand and let the ball drop into the red dirt. The fans let out a sea of cheers that poured on the field and lifted Tía Berta and our mother. I looked at Rosana, and she turned to me and said softly, "Mom is the best," and it echoed through every ballpark in the world.

The Crash Room

When my brother Roger and I were growing up, people would ask each of us, "What do you want to be when you grow up?" They weren't asking us if we wanted to be sad or happy or mean or loving; they just wanted to know what kind of work we wanted to do.

It's really a crazy question to ask a five- and six-year-old. But it became a way to compete with each other. To see who could best impress the grownup.

We'd look up at the inquisitive adult and let one of our inner whispers shout out. Roger was quick to shout "football player," but he instead became a track star in high school and then later, when he joined the army, one of the fastest soldiers in his battalion.

I would shout out one of the following with zest: race car driver, jet pilot, astronaut! And at the time I think I meant it, but at the age of eight I saw and touched a dead man. His cool silence killed the blasting engines of cars, planes, and rocket ships. The whisper word was now "doctor."

My mother was and still is an x-ray technologist, but over twenty-five years ago she was a housekeeper at Knapp Memorial Hospital in Weslaco, Texas. It was the hospital I was born in and the place where Mom cleaned bathrooms and the radiology department. A woman named Irene told my mother that she could be more than just a housekeeper and taught my mom how to x-ray fingers and toes.

After two years at Knapp, Mom got a job at Edinburg General Hospital decontaminating and sterilizing surgical instruments. The woman who hired my mother and a doctor who saw her potential took it upon themselves to train her to be an x-ray technologist. After six months of training, Mom was on her own and held the job title X-Ray Technologist.

We lived in a town called Edcouch, which was about twelve miles away from Edinburg. The hospital was small, about fifty beds, and did not have a round-the-clock x-ray staff, so the techs took turns taking graveyard call.

Highway 107 between Edcouch and Edinburg had no street-lights and was surrounded by nothing but fields of cabbage, corn, carrots, and cotton. Mom would always take me with her instead of Roger, who shared my father's discomfort. Anytime we had to drop off something for Mom at the hospital, Dad and Roger stayed in the car and sent me in because they would simply get nervous around folks in lab coats.

When Dad went through boot camp, he passed out when they gave him his shots, and Roger couldn't stand the sight of blood. One time we all went to see *Night of the Living Dead* over at a drive-in theater, and neither Dad nor Roger would get out of the car to get some refreshments. They didn't even like going to the cemetery to put flowers on the graves of relatives.

Mom and I, on the other hand, weren't afraid of hospitals or doctors, and I wanted to be a surgeon. I thought that blood was fascinating and that dead bodies were especially cool. And so when Mom was on call, I didn't mind at all losing a couple of hours of sleep.

An ER nurse would phone Mom at odd hours of the night and tell her what kind of x-ray they needed, which determined how fast we had to drive. On those late-night commutes I would be wide awake, driving with Mom, heading toward Edinburg General Hospital. I was Robin next to Batman, speeding in the Batmobile.

I got to see quite a bit and, in the process, I learned medical terminology, the names of bones in the body, and how to develop x-ray film. I would share my hospital stories with my brother, but he wasn't impressed. He would say I was weird or, worse yet, say things like, "I'll bet you look real cute in a white dress." I would chase him, but he was too fast.

When I was fifteen years old, we moved to Austin, and Mom got a job at the Brackenridge Hospital. At the time, it was the only hospital with a trauma center (called the crash room), which also served the city and county. It was a busy place, too busy for me to go and hang around. But soon I was old enough to apply for a job there.

I was seventeen, and the job was to be a patient transporter for the radiology department. It took a month before I was called in for an interview. In the meantime I worked in a fast food restaurant frying fish.

At school my brother joined the track team and had girls chasing him all over the place. I joined a club for students interested in the medical field and had no girls chasing me. Our sponsor was the school nurse, whom I put down as one of my references, and so I got the job. Of course, having Mom work in the department helped, too.

It was great. I went down with Mom to a hospital uniform supply store and got a couple of white lab coats. When I got home I modeled for the family, but Roger said that I'd probably look better in a dress and laughed. I snapped back, "You wait till you're dying in a hospital and I have to save your neck!" My mom and dad got mad and said I shouldn't say such things, but Roger told them not to worry because I'd never be a doctor.

On the first three days of work, Brackenridge put me through an intense orientation, took a photograph for my hospital badge, and trained me in CPR. I thought I looked pretty cool, walking down the hospital halls with my lab coat and badge. I could see myself as Dr. Eduardo Cuellar Aguilar one day. I was the youngest in the department, but I learned fast and worked hard.

Within weeks of starting work at Brackenridge, I became well acquainted with the x-ray darkroom, memorized the file codes of the x-ray jackets, learned all the departments, knew my way around all nine floors, and knew the names of many of the hospital staff from the housekeepers to the attractive nurses.

I was happy at Brackenridge. The pay was good and I worked only on weekends, which was when all the action came in. I worked twelve to sixteen hours every Saturday and Sunday, and I didn't mind.

X-ray was next to ER, and during the weekends the x-ray staff spent half of their time in there. We had two portable x-ray machines in ER, and both were used every hour. I was a runner between the departments, going back and forth with x-ray film cassettes. I would assist the tech setting up the shot by lifting the patient into position and then standing back with my fifteen-pound lead apron on. A beep would sound out and I would take the cassette back to x-ray, develop the film, and return to ER with another cassette, in case the doctor didn't like the way the film came out.

Portables were done not only in ER but on any floor where the patient was too ill to come down, or if his limbs were surrounded in plaster casts with stainless steel pins sticking out all over the place and cords with weights on the ends, keeping his arms or legs in proper position. Many times these patients looked like human TV antennas or sad string puppets. The intensive care and cardiac care units had their own portables, and whenever I had the time, I would tag along with a tech to do a portable.

There were always tubes and wires to watch out for when doing portables. Most of the patients would have at least an I.V. going and many had catheters and heart monitors. The floor nurses were sometimes too busy to help the techs with the patient, so my tagging along was appreciated.

There was a small department at Brackenridge made up of kids who just did transporting, but they didn't see as much as I did. They were my age and went to different high schools. Most were the sons and daughters of physicians. When I first met them, they asked if my father or mother was a doctor; they were sort of snobby.

One of them, Jim, was the son of the county medical examiner, and when someone died in ER or on one of the floors, Jim had no problem transporting the body to the hospital morgue, which was in the basement of the old hospital.

Jim and I became good friends, and he would call me whenever he had to transport a body down to the morgue. If his father were there, we could walk around and ask all sorts of questions. Going to the morgue always involved a spooky walk through a couple of long, dim halls, and Jim didn't like to admit that the trip, especially with a dead body by your side, was scary.

There was a way to get there by going through the first floor, but there were usually too many patient visitors walking around, and the dead do deserve respect. Instead we always got into the service elevator and pressed two buttons at the same time to bypass all the floors and get to the basement without stopping. The basement was an eerie place filled with machines dotted with red and green lights and huge metal pipes that clung to walls and hung from the ceiling, that snaked their way along and grew more numerous as we guided the corpse through the maze to yet another elevator.

The second elevator was small, with just enough room for the stretcher on one side and Jim and me on the other. We said out loud, "The living on this side, the dead on that side!" We went up one floor, and the door would open to a view of a beautiful enclosed courtyard, almost a garden. There was a picnic bench in the center, shaded by three big pecan trees standing in a slow breeze and surrounded by lush green Saint Augustine grass. Then down one long covered sidewalk with only half a wall, so you were practically outside, and voilà, the morgue.

It was a small room that smelled of formaldehyde, and in the center of the room was a permanent stainless-steel table. More often than not, there would be a nude body on the table. Illustrations of human anatomy covered the walls, and pens, clipboards, and forms with the seal of Texas were scattered on the two desks of the medical examiners.

When Jim's father was there, he would give a little synopsis of their latest case, and sometimes, if he was in the middle of an autopsy, we'd get a quick lesson in anatomy. At the back of the morgue were the stainless-steel refrigerators, no different from the ones in detective movies. They opened like file cabinets, but inside they were cold. We'd pull out one of the empty drawers and lift the body onto the cold metal, sometimes making little jokes as we closed the door. One time we opened the wrong drawer and there was a dead man's body with his right elbow bent, putting his hand in the air. Jim and I pushed the arm down, but it just jerked right back up. We thought it was funny.

The best thing about working at the hospital was that I got to help people. I tried to follow the golden rule. If patients were cold (and you know how cold hospitals are), I would give them a blanket. If they looked real cold or were elderly, they got heated blankets.

It was cool when the doctors in ER asked for me. Since I spoke Spanish, I could translate for them. I would go into ER and talk to the patients and try to make them more comfortable, because being a patient is no fun, especially if you don't understand a word of what is being said all around you. I imagined it must be like being abducted by a UFO.

I was thrilled about surgery and the trauma rooms. Although I never got a chance to watch any surgeries, I did see much in the crash room, where a ballet of lab and x-ray techs, nurses, and doctors took place whenever a patient came in.

In order to be a patient in the crash room, you had to be a Code Three. There were four types of codes. Code One meant you may not feel well, so you'll just have to sit until we get to you, and in the meantime you'll see people who make your petty pain feel silly. Code Two meant that you're probably bleeding and you went ahead of Code One. Code Three was serious, because you are a mess. The crash room was created for folks who may not make it. Code Three was the center of the dance. Code Four meant you were dead. The ambulance drivers would be speeding to Brackenridge with the Code Three patient, and the crash team would be getting ready, but then the drivers would radio in a Code Four and the team would stand down.

But when a Code Three came in, with the patient holding on for dear life, people would be flying in and out of the crash room. Most of the time there would be blood all over the floor, and the medical staff left footprints in blood all over the ER and down the halls.

Nurses would simply tear away at the packages containing medical equipment and throw the trash on the floor. Everyone had a duty; IVs were started, heart monitors put in place, x-rays were taken, doctors specializing in whatever the main problem was would shout out orders, and people moved—not for the doctors, mind you, but for the patient. It was a rush.

I saw one person die in the crash room and others who died hours or days later. Many times the patient would go straight to surgery from the crash room and the wheels of the stretcher left blood trails. Sometimes I would help lift the patient, and blood would drench the latex gloves that covered my hands. Watching someone else's blood drip down from my fingers to the floor always made me think that somehow it was my blood.

After two years at Brackenridge I began not to like myself. I had become rather insensitive to people's pain and suffering. If I saw someone crying about his minor pains, I would say things like, "Oh, quit your whining." It was an attitude I had picked up from others in the department and throughout the hospital. Especially if they were drunk patients, or were doing stupid things just to show off. Those folks could just sit and wait in the cold hall, and they were lucky if they even got a blanket.

However, this insensitivity was affecting my entire personality. At school I was beginning to have difficulty making friends and keeping girlfriends. Girls I liked said I was callous, and Roger was considered the sweet brother, while I was the jerk brother.

Worse yet, I didn't feel like being a doctor anymore. I didn't see what good all this medicine and medical equipment were doing. Every now and then I would get happy about some patient making a wonderful recovery, but usually it was only because their family members were there every day to support them. The elderly seemed to die alone many times. The whole place was depressing me.

I used to visit one man, who reminded me of my grandfather, every Saturday and Sunday. He was there for three weeks, and on the third weekend when I went up to see him, he wasn't in his room. I thought, "Great, he's outta here, he's well." I went to the nurse's station and asked if he had been moved or if he recovered. The nurse looked at me and said rather nonchalantly, "Oh no, honey, he died a few days ago." I tried to look cool, said thanks, and walked down the hall. But once I was in the elevator, I felt weak and was depressed the rest of the day, thinking to myself that I should have paid him a visit during the week.

Now the only place in the hospital I enjoyed going to was the garden in the old part of the hospital. Just about every time I worked I would go there and sit on the picnic table alone, and eat my lunch, watching the squirrels chase each other. One day as I sat in the garden I saw Jim wheeling a dead body across the hall toward the morgue. He smiled and waved at me.

"Hey," I said.

He stopped and stood upright from his hunched position. "Guess who this is?"

"Someone dead?" I said with a shrug of my shoulders.

He laughed. "Yeah. It's that guy who was hit by that eighteen-wheeler last week. You know, the guy with the twin baby girls."

I nodded. "What a drag," I said.

"Yeah. Hey, I'll be right out in a minute," Jim said.

I waved back. "OK."

I looked back across the garden and saw some baby squirrels playing and thought about those baby twins playing alone. Then I looked at the windows of the old hospital where I knew the obstetrics unit was. I realized then that the only way to get out of my depression was to watch a baby being born.

I didn't wait for Jim to come back out. He still thought taking bodies to the morgue was fun, and I didn't care to hear the gruesome details of the man's death.

I wrapped the rest of my sandwich and walked over to the OB unit, and asked the nurses if they would call me to watch a birth. It took about three weeks, but eventually I had the chance to watch a baby take its first breath.

One Sunday morning I was taking a woman who was in the last stages of her labor up to OB. The nurse told me that she would ask the doctor if I could watch the delivery, and he said it was fine with him, but I had only a minute and a half to get into scrubs and mask. I jumped at the chance, dressed fast, and was in the room with my eyes wide open.

The doctor asked the woman, who was in the middle of delivering her baby, if I could assist him. It was crazy. Here was this woman giving birth—she was in real pain, not like those macho men coming in for x-rays of sprained ankles caused by playing tag football or softball—and she lifted her head up slightly and nodded; she couldn't have cared less. I said thank you through my mask. It was an incredible moment for me. A baby boy was born, looking no different from me when I was born. I could hear my heart pumping and I felt as if I could almost see God; that's how strange yet spiritual the whole thing was.

The rest of the week I was on clouds, but I knew that I had to quit this job. To leave with new blood speeding through me. Two weeks after the birth, I put in my resignation notice. My mother told me that it was a good job, that I should stay, but I didn't feel like watching people die. It seemed to me that no matter what doctors did to save patients, they would eventually die and I didn't want a job like that.

Six years later, my mother was working in a different hospital, and I was dating Marie, who had been an x-ray tech at Brackenridge when I worked there. Marie worked at yet another hospital. Brackenridge was now just a big hospital off Interstate 35, and when I drove by it, I was glad I wasn't there.

But one Christmas season, after I had married Marie, we found ourselves standing in the Brackenridge ER crash room, next to my brother Roger, who lay dying on a stretcher. I was dazed as I stood there. Marie held my hand to give me hope, but we had seen Roger's CAT scan, and he was a mess. He wasn't going anywhere except down to the basement, through the darkness and into the garden.

We knew most of the medical staff, some of whom were even at our wedding, and they all expressed their sorrow. I knew they had done their best because the crash room floor was littered with wrappers and covered in blood. It was a bad auto accident that Roger had been in, leaving him brain-dead. Beautiful smooth brown skin covered his athletic twenty-four-year-old body that now lived only through machines. His soul was ready to fly.

I spoke to him. I told him he was in the crash room. I told him that this was serious stuff, to quit playing around. But Roger never listened to me. He would just walk away with a wave of his hand. But I held his hand tight, wanting him to stay.

His death changed my Me. At the wake his friends from the army and his countless girlfriends talked about how fast he was. How he ran every day, no matter what the weather. He was training to be the fastest in his division and was a mere second behind the leader. If he could be the fastest, then I could be a doctor.

Medical school wasn't easy for me, but I studied every day. I imagined I was in a race and that becoming a doctor was crossing the finishing line. When things got hard I pretended Roger was there, urging me on as I did him at his track meets.

I now walk the halls of the hospital with a white lab coat on and stethoscope around my neck and a badge that says Dr. Eduardo Cuellar Aguilar. When I work my shift in ER and hear the ambulance drivers say they have a Code Three coming in, I feel the blood rushing into my legs for a race I always want to win.

One Morning Fishing

It's not easy being a father. A father has to compete with other fathers as in "My daddy is bigger than your daddy." "Oh yeah? Well, my daddy can beat up your daddy." Fathers can usually compete with other fathers, but to compete against TV fathers Ward Cleaver, Dr. Alex Stone, and all-time champion Andy Taylor is sometimes too much.

When I was eight years old, my father took my younger brother Roger and me fishing mainly because Andy Taylor took Opie fishing. Dad did everything he could to be a good father. He showed interest in everything my brother and I did. We joined the Boy Scouts; Dad joined the Boy Scouts; we became junior volunteer firemen; Dad became a volunteer fireman. Whatever sport we played, Dad would attend all the games and cheer regardless of how much time we spent on the bench. So when Roger and I wanted to go fishing, Dad took us fishing.

On Saturday morning Roger and I were up early so we could watch the best cartoons. It was close to eight when Dad told us we had to leave soon to get a good fishing spot. Dad didn't own any fishing equipment, so we had to buy all our fishing gear. He got Mom up so she could make some tacos for us to eat. Mom made extra tacos and wrapped them in foil paper for us to eat later, and she packed some Hunt's snack-pack pudding. With our lunches and a jug of water we were ready to go fishing. Roger and I hopped into Dad's yellow Ford Galaxy 500, and off we went to Delta Lake.

It was a man-made lake just past a small town called Monte Alto about six miles from our hometown of Edcouch. Delta Lake wasn't deep blue or crystal clear like lakes on postcards. It was a murky dark green with patches of brown here and there. Some of the trees submerged in the water could still be seen. Their dead, bare branches were rotten and black and looked like the fingers of unseen hands. Attempting to water-ski on Delta Lake would be stupid because of the trees, but then nobody skied on the lake because nobody owned a ski boat.

It was a scary lake. Over twelve people had drowned in it, with one death caused by some mysterious amoeba. There were big white signs all around the lake with red letters: DANGER. SWIMMING IS NOT ALLOWED IN DELTA LAKE. This warning was written in English and Spanish. To top it off, the sign also had an illustration of a skull and crossbones like the kind seen on bottles containing poison. I doubt that Delta Lake is on any postcards. It wasn't the best of lakes, but it was all we had. Besides, we weren't planning to eat the fish we caught. None of us liked fish or, for that matter, any other type of seafood.

On the way to Delta Lake, Dad played his favorite eight-track tape, the one of Credence Clearwater Revival. It was CCR's greatest hits, and Roger and I loved to sing along. Our favorite was "Out My Back Door," which was about animals playing in a band. One of the lines went like this: "Tambourines and elephants are playing in the band." But Roger and I always sang, "Tangerines and elephants are playing in the band." Every time we sang that line wrong, which was every time Dad played it, he would laugh and correct us, but we'd just do it again.

Once we got to the lake we stopped at the only store there, Delta Lake Store, but it was closed and didn't open until nine o'clock, so we drove around the lake to see if there were any good fishing spots left. Delta Lake was surrounded by a gravel road just wide enough for two cars to pass each other. As we drove, we could see lots of fishing spots since there was no one else around. Halfway around the lake, I asked Dad if I could eat my Hunt's snack-pack pudding, but before Dad could respond, Roger added, "Yeah, Dad, can we eat our pudding, please?"

"If you eat your pudding now you won't have any when you eat your lunch," Dad said.

"Aw, come on, Dad, please," I said, giving him my best puppy-eyes look. Roger looked even more puppy-eyed. Roger and I never worked on anything together unless there was a strong incentive; chocolate pudding always brought our stomachs together. By the time we had circled the lake once, the Delta Lake Store was open.

As we entered, the man sitting behind a glass counter, who was reading a gun magazine, said, "Mornin'." He was an older white man and wore a white cap and red suspenders. He sat in one of those aluminum-frame lawn chairs.

The glass counter in front of him was filled with half-empty boxes of chocolate bars, gum, candy, and fishing hooks. One of the walls was covered with fishing poles and with baseball caps of all sizes and colors. On the opposite wall were refrigerator cases full of soda and beer.

In the center, the store was divided by a shelf with cookies, chips, cans of food, and toilet paper. A fine layer of dust covered everything in the store. There were Zebco fishing poles wrapped in plastic, ready to use. Twelve ninety-nine each and they came in two tones, blue and white.

We also bought some little gray weights and red-and-white cone-shaped floaters. I guess they were called floaters. Anyway, we needed some bait, and there were all types of live and dead slimy-looking bait. The man behind the counter asked Dad what kind of bait he wanted, but Dad was not sure.

"What's the best bait?" Dad asked.

"That depends what ya fishing for," the man said, slightly lifting his cap. Dad shrugged his shoulders.

"I don't know. What . . ."

"Catfish!" Roger shouted.

"Roger!" Dad snapped, then regained his composure. "Ah, yeah. We want to catch some catfish," Dad said in a half-confident voice, but the man didn't look impressed. The man pointed to some red, wormy-looking bait and said that was what catfish liked. So Dad bought half a pound of the red worms and some shrimp as well, but before we left the store, we convinced Dad to buy us some Cokes and Hershey chocolate bars. We were ready to catch the biggest catfish alive in Delta Lake.

Dad found the perfect fishing spot, and we were the only people around. Alone on the lake, just Dad, Roger, and me.

It took some time to get our fishing poles ready since none of us really knew how to fish. Roger and I didn't want to touch the worms because they were covered with blood, but Dad said worms didn't have blood. Dad tried to get the worms on the hooks, but they kept falling off.

So he decided to use the shrimp because they were easier to stab. Roger and I didn't mind touching the shrimp, because they were blood-free. We cast out our lines and waited for the fish to start biting. Dad left the stereo on in the car and opened the doors so we could listen to CCR while we fished.

After sitting in the Valley morning sun for about five minutes, the brotherly bond formed by the pudding was melting fast.

"Dad, do fish bite?" Roger asked, but before Dad could answer, I said, "Fish don't bite, zonzo."

"Sharks bite and killer whales too," Roger fired back.

"Yeah, well, there aren't any sharks and killer whales in Delta Lake, zonzo!"

"That's enough from both of you, and don't call your brother a zonzo," Dad said.

"Yeah, but . . ."

"Be quiet! You're going to scare the fish away if you keep talking."

"How can they hear us? They're under water," I said.

"I didn't know fish had ears," Roger said.

"You're going to scare the fish away if you keep making noise."

"But, Dad, you have the radio on and it's louder than us," I said.

By now Dad was irritated. "David! Roger! Listen. Just reel in your lines to see if you caught anything."

So we reeled in our lines to find nothing and both our shrimps were gone. Dad said the shrimp had fallen off. So we put some more bait on our hooks and tried again. Each time we reeled in our lines to see if we had caught any fish, the shrimps were gone. Each time we put the shrimps back on the hook and tried a different way of baiting the hook, but we still kept losing our shrimps. After twenty minutes of shrimp losing, we finally lost our desire to catch the big one.

"Dad, can we go home now?" Roger asked.

"Yeah, Dad, I'm ready, too. Besides, we don't even like fish."

Looking back now, I realize Dad couldn't wait to hear those words come out of our mouths.

"Are you sure? We still have lots of bait left, and it's not even lunchtime."

All we could do was nod yes.

"OK, then. Reel in your lines so we can go."

We reeled in our baitless lines, and Dad threw the red worms and remaining shrimps into the lake. That made Roger and me happy because the bait smelled bad, and we didn't want to ride in the car with it. When we put the fishing equipment in the trunk of the car, we noticed that Dad had brought our BB guns and a box of BBs, so we spent an hour shooting at Coke cans. Roger and I tried to see who could hit the middle of the letter "o" in the word "Coke."

When we got back to Edcouch, Mom couldn't believe we were home so early.

"Did you catch any fish?" Mom asked, hoping we hadn't because she didn't like fish either.

"No, our dumb bait kept falling off," Roger said.

"Yeah, besides, we don't like fish anyway," I said. Dad went straight to the TV to watch the Cowboys, and Roger and I ran down to our friend's house to show him our new fishing poles.

Empty Corner

The quick jab to his jaw rattled his brain. It felt as if his eyes were spinning in their sockets as his mouthpiece shot out, covered in saliva and blood. Coach Garza, standing outside the corner of the ring, knew this would happen. Marcos just couldn't help picking on a smaller fighter, especially one who did not like to fight.

"That's enough, Marcos. Alex, you all right?"

Coach Garza knelt beside Alex, trying to help him up. Alex didn't even know he was on the canvas, but there he was, looking up at the coach.

"You all right? Feel OK?"

"Ah, Coach! He's just being a baby. I barely hit him," Marcos said.

"Like hell, Marcos! I told you to go easy and to spar with him, not to fight him!"

"He's just being a baby, Coach," Marcos repeated.

Coach didn't have much patience, and Marcos didn't understand reasoning very well, so Coach Garza used what Marcos understood best: aggression. The coach stood up to his full six feet and walked over to Marcos's five-foot-ten frame.

"OK, Marcos, you want to spar with me like you sparred with Alex? Do you? Because if you want, I'll get my gloves on right now and we'll go a couple of rounds, and I'll spar with you just like you sparred with Alex."

Marcos stood silent, not making much eye contact with Coach Garza, just like a dog when it's being scolded by its master.

"Yeah, Coach, but you're bigger than me and stronger."

Coach Garza shook his head. It seemed Marcos always had an excuse.

"Marcos, shut up! Go hit the showers," Coach said.

Coach Garza stared at Marcos until Marcos disappeared down the hall. Alex was sitting up now but still felt a little light-headed. His eyes had stopped spinning, and the gym was now upright. Coach Garza extended his hand and helped Alex up.

"You're going to be OK. You just got a small cut on your lip," Coach said.

Alex got up and felt a little better. At least the coach didn't yell at him or call him some name for falling down.

"Thanks, Coach. I feel better."

"You sure you're OK?"

"Yeah, yeah, I feel better," Alex said.

"Bueno, hit the showers," Coach said.

He didn't feel better, though. He was still a little dizzy from the blow Marcos had given him, and he just wanted to go home. He walked slowly to the showers, hoping that Marcos would not be there, but there he was, already dressed to go and waiting for Alex. Alex hated confronting Marcos. Marcos stood up as Alex entered the locker room, his chest out and fist clenched. Marcos looked mean and he knew that he scared Alex. He walked up to Alex just as Coach Garza had done to him earlier.

"Pinche güey. You're lucky the Coach is here to save your ass, but if I see you on the street or . . ."

Suddenly Coach Garza appeared at the entrance. "If you see Alex on the street, what are you going to do, Marcos, eh? I'll tell you what you're going to do—nothing! You understand? Because if you bother Alex outside the gym and I hear about it, I'll tell your parents that you can't come here anymore, and I won't train you anymore. You understand that, Marcos? Do you?" Coach asked.

Once again Marcos became the obedient dog and said nothing.

"Do you understand? Yes or no?" Coach demanded.

"Yeah, Coach," Marcos answered.

"No, Marcos. Yes or no," Coach said.

"Yes, Coach."

"I can't hear you."

"Yes, I understand, Coach."

Coach Garza stood still staring at Marcos, his chest raised and both hands on his hips.

"Bueno. Now go home, and we'll see you tomorrow at four-thirty on the dot," Coach said.

Coach Garza had saved Alex for the hundredth time this month, and Alex hadn't even fought in a real fight yet.

Coach Garza liked Alex. Alex was smart, not stupid like Marcos. Coach Garza had had high hopes for Marcos at one time, but he turned out to be a stupid bully like others he had trained before. Alex, though, could be a good fighter, maybe even a great fighter. Alex was a southpaw, and Coach knew he could train him to win fights. It would just take some time and a little patience. But one thing was certain: Coach Garza was going to make a fighter out of him, one way or another.

"Bueno, Alex, hit the showers and don't worry about Marcos. He's just jealous because he knows one day you'll be a great boxer and he won't amount to nothing," Coach said with a slight nod.

Alex felt better knowing Coach was there to help him with Marcos. And it felt good to know that Coach believed in him. But Alex knew he would never be a great boxer. He had never wanted to be a boxer; it was his father's idea. Alex had told his father he didn't like boxing, but his father wouldn't listen. His father would tell Alex to be a man and not act like his sisters.

As the hot water flowed over Alex's fourteen-year-old body, he relaxed. The water stung the open wound on his lip, and his head still echoed from the jab, but at least he was out of the ring. Two months had passed and he still did not like boxing. His stomach growled as he thought about his mother's cooking and wondered what she might have to eat at home.

Alex's house was warm with the aroma of Spanish rice, beans, and tortillas. His mother tended to the cooking, and his three sisters set the table, the women flowing from table to stove in a dance that neither Alex nor his father had learned. Whenever Alex or his father wandered into the kitchen, they would only step on feet and disrupt the women's dance.

Once everyone was seated and served, the family would begin a discussion that would eventually end up in a dispute. Verónica, the oldest sister, like everyone else at the table, noticed Alex's swollen lip.

"Alejandro, what happened to your lip?" Verónica asked.

Alex took a deep breath and began to utter the first word in his sentence, but the sound was drowned out by his father.

"¡Nada pasó! It's just a little cut. Boxers get cuts on the lip all the time," his father said.

"Well, that's pretty big for a little cut," Verónica replied.

Verónica was the one in college and was considered the smartest one in the family. She knew Alex didn't like boxing and would try to protect him from her father's machismo.

"What? You can hardly see it," their father said.

"Well, at least you didn't get a black eye or a broken jaw," María said, the baby of the family. "Who punched you?"

"Marcos did," Alex said.

"Marcos! Marcos is a jerk and a bully and ugly. Nobody at school likes him," Suzanna said, making a face of disgust.

"One day, Alex, you'll be big enough to beat him up," María said with music in her voice.

Alex began to smile, but he could feel his lip open, and the salt from the hot rice stung.

"Well, he'll never beat up anybody if he doesn't take his boxing seriously," his father said.

"Well, maybe he shouldn't be taking boxing lessons," Verónica said. "I mean, Alex doesn't even like boxing, and what good is it anyway? Right, Alex?"

Alex said nothing; he just looked at the white tablecloth. It covered the table in a flower pattern filled with holes. He could see the bare, brown table underneath, thinking of how crumbs always managed to get under the tablecloth.

"Tell him, Alex," Verónica urged him.

"Verónica, would you let your brother talk for once!" Alex's father snapped. "You're always interrupting everybody. You never let anybody talk. Now, Alex, is it true you want to quit?"

Alex looked at Verónica, who nodded slightly as if to say, "Go on." Then he looked at his other two sisters, who were afraid Alex was going to say that he didn't want to box anymore. Then there was his mother, who looked tired of the whole affair. Alex looked at his father.

The room became the ring he hated. In this corner of the table sat the challenger, Alex. Weighing in at 120 pounds and holding no titles. And in that corner sat the undefeated champion, Alex's father. Weighing in at 215 pounds, his father, the man of the house and king of the casa.

"Yeah, Dad, I don't want to box anymore," Alex said.

"What! Why not? Coach Garza says you're getting better all the time, and he thinks you can be a great fighter," his father said. "Is Marcos bothering you? Because if he is, I'll talk to Coach Garza and he'll straighten him out."

Alex thought for a moment that he could use Marcos as an excuse, but knew it would just cause more problems.

"No, no one is bothering me," he said, shaking his head. "I just don't like it. I'd rather play soccer or something else."

"You don't like it! Well, you're not going to like it when someone beats you up!" his father burst out. "How's soccer going to help you in a fight? Eh?"

Alex's mother, the only person who could silence her husband, finally spoke.

"¡Ya! Por favor, Roberto, ¡déjalo!" she said in a raised voice as if she were scolding one of the children. "If he doesn't want to box then he doesn't have to! Si quieres, *you* take boxing lessons."

The family was silent for a second, then Alex's father spoke.

"You do what you want. Pero when you get into a fight and get beat up, don't come crying to me." With that, Alex's father got up and left the room. The rest of the family sat in silence looking at each other and in unison exhaled in relief. "¡Ese hombre!" Alex's mother said in frustration.

"Why is he that way? He's always getting mad about something," Verónica said. "Well, Alex, it looks like you finally won one."

Alex said nothing. He nodded slowly as if to agree with Verónica, but he didn't know that this was just round one.

The following day Alex was a little happier knowing he didn't have to box. After school he walked home with some stride in his step. He watched television, trying to find something he liked. Alex looked at the clock on the wall showing the time was four-thirty. Right at this time, if he were still in training, he would be stretching so he could begin doing push-ups and sit-ups until it hurt. Alex was happy he wasn't at the gym. Just then the phone rang. He answered it, recognizing the voice almost immediately. It was Coach Garza.

"Hey, Alex, it's four-thirty. Why aren't you here?" he asked.

"Hey, Coach, uh . . . well, you see, I don't want to box anymore, Coach."

"Now listen, Alex, your father called me last night and told me you didn't want to train anymore, and I think I know why," Coach said. "It's Marcos, right?"

"No, Coach, it's . . ."

"Look, Alex, I know he likes to pick on you, but he won't be picking on you anymore, OK? I told Marcos he'll have to find another trainer, so it'll be just you and me from now on. What do you say?"

Alex was glad that Coach wasn't mad at him, but he just didn't want to train anymore. How was he going to tell Coach without making him mad, especially after all his patience and now getting rid of Marcos, too?

"Come on, Alex. You're almost there," Coach continued.

"Maybe later, Coach. Next year or something, but I just need some time off to think about it, you know?"

"Alex, the more time you take off, the more out of shape you'll get, and it'll be twice as hard to get you back into shape," Coach said. "And besides, boxing will keep you in shape for soccer when the season starts."

Alex thought again for a moment. "Coach, let me think about it . . ."

"Listen, Alex, boxing can also help you in a fight," Coach continued.

"I know, Coach, I know, but if you can just give me some time, OK?"

"All right, Alex, I'll give you some time to think about it, but when you are ready just let me know, OK?"

"Thanks, Coach."

Alex was glad that was over. Now he could go on with other things and not worry about boxing.

The following weeks were good for Alex. His father was speaking to him and not making as many comments as before. Comments such as "Since you aren't doing anything now, why don't you help your sisters in the kitchen?" or "Did you get into a fight today? Because when you do, you'll see."

One afternoon Alex stayed late at school so he could attend a soccer club meeting. His father said he would pick him up around five-thirty. The meeting was over at five o'clock, and Alex sat on the steps of the school waiting. At five-thirty his father had not shown up yet, but it was typical for him to be late. He called home and no one answered. At six o'clock Alex assumed that his father had forgotten, and not wanting to wait, he began walking home.

Alex walked home thinking about soccer, and every now and then kicked a can or a rock with the side of his foot. He stopped at a store to call home, but again there was no answer.

It was starting to get dark, and Alex could see the fluorescent lights in the shopping centers and gas stations. All he needed was to pass one more convenience store, and then he would be in his neighborhood, only a few blocks from home.

As he passed the dumpster of the convenience store, he felt a hard slap on his right arm and then a quick, tight grip. Before Alex could look at his attacker, he was jerked behind the dumpster and hit squarely in the face. One hard blow followed another and another. The punches made him see bright electrical storms flashing through his brain. Who could this be but Marcos? He thought for a second. Alex tried to wrap his arms around the person just as he would do in training, but when he did, he received a blow to his stomach. Alex gasped for air as he began to fall, but the person was strong and wouldn't let Alex hit the ground, holding him up for another hit that finally made him drop to the pavement.

Alex opened his eyes and saw the headlights of a car shining on him, and someone was trying to talk to him. He knew he was hurt because his face was numb, and it was difficult for him to keep his eyes open. The person asked questions. "You all right? Can you talk? What's your name and where do you live?" Alex slowly sat up with the woman's help; she sounded like his sister, but she wasn't. All he could tell was that she had dark hair and was wearing jeans. He wiped his mouth on his shirt, and the blood looked black under the yellow street lamps.

Alex told her that he didn't live far from the store and asked if she would give him a ride home. When they arrived at Alex's home, he tried to thank her and tell her that he could make it just fine from there, but the words were not coming out, the numbness was wearing off, and the pain was beginning to pulsate.

She walked him to the front door and rang the doorbell. Alex kept his head down and lightly leaned on the woman. His mother answered the doorbell. Alex looked up at her.

"Ay Dios, Alejandro. ¿Qué te pasó?" she said as the blood rushed from her face.

Alex said nothing; he only sighed, trying to figure out how he was going to explain what he didn't understand.

"Someone was attacking him or something at the store down the street," said the woman who was with him. "I didn't get to see him, really. He ran off when I drove up."

Now all four women were at the door, taking Alex and the woman into the house; they gathered around him, each of them having some physical contact with him.

"What happened, now?" Verónica asked, as if she were the official historian of the family. The woman explained how she had seen a man attacking Alex at the store, and that he ran off when she drove up.

"Did you get a good look at him?" Verónica asked.

"No, it was dark and he was already running away as I drove up."

As she finished speaking, the headlights of a car flashed across Alex's house. His father's car pulled into the driveway. He knew what his father was going to say, as did the women of the house. They all paused and looked at the headlights and heard the engine shut off.

"Great. That's all we need," Verónica said.

The woman who brought Alex could sense the tension building. She knew that something was about to start, and she didn't want to be there when it did.

"Ah, if you will excuse me, I really need to be going."

"Thank you for all that you have done. You have been very kind," Verónica said with a polite smile as she walked the woman out. The woman took the thank-you and left quickly.

Alex's head throbbed and it hurt so much that all he could hear was a sharp ringing sound. His sisters laid him down on the sofa, and one of them wiped his cuts and bruises with a warm cloth. His father came into the house and knew something had happened.

"Who was that woman? What's going on here, eh?"

Alex's mother looked at him, knowing that there was no easy way to tell him what had happened to Alex.

Verónica spoke up. "Someone beat him up! So there! Are you happy now?" she said as if he were to blame. "That's what you wanted, right? So he would have to take those damn boxing lessons again, right?"

"Well, he would have been fine if he was still boxing! This never would have happened!" her father shouted. "See, I told you this would happen. But not one of you would listen. Especially you, Verónica, and now your brother has been beaten up because of you!"

"¡Ya, Roberto! ¿Por qué eres así? Your son is hurt! He doesn't need to hear your lectures now," said Alex's mother in anger.

Alex felt like crying but he couldn't because he was mad at himself and mad that his father was right.

"Ya, that's enough. I just want to go to my room. Please, I can take care of myself," Alex said as he began to get up. He kept looking down, not wanting his family to see his face. Alex's mother put her hand to his chin and lifted it slightly. She noticed that his lips were cut in two places and his eyes were swelling. She felt terrible for Alex. "Ay, mijo," she said.

Alex's mother and sisters surrounded him with soft voices as Alex walked toward his room. María had tears in her eyes, and Suzanna put her arm around María's shoulder to keep her from crying. The wife glanced at her husband with hate as she walked her son away.

Alex's father stood alone in the room listening to the voices fade. He felt that maybe he should say something kind to Alex but instead walked into the kitchen, took a beer out of the refrigerator, twisted off the cap, and took a drink. The coolness of the bottle and the taste of the beer soothed his racing blood. He took another drink, then reached for the telephone to dial the number he'd been dialing so often the week before. An answering machine came on.

"Hello, this is Ron Garza. Thanks for calling but I'm not home right now. But if you leave a message and a phone number, I'll get back to you as soon as I can."

The beep sounded for a few seconds. "Hello, Coach Garza, this is Roberto Reyes, Alex's father. I think your idea worked. Maybe Alex will start training again next week. Don't call me, I'll call you."

He hung up the telephone and took another drink. He sat down on a chair and rubbed his knuckles, wondering if his son would ever know how much he loved him.

El Sapo

Ro one could throw a frog as high as I could. Not even Orlando Álvarez, who was taller and stronger, could throw a sapo higher. See, I knew how to hold a sapo right. Just like throwing a terremote, except a sapo doesn't fall apart in the air.

Finding sapos was easy in my neighborhood. I lived in Edcouch, Texas, a small town in the Rio Grande Valley just one hour from the Gulf of Mexico, and when it rained, it rained long and hard. After a good hard rain, the ditches in front of our frame houses would fill up. The dirt from the gravel roads would follow the rain into the ditches, making the water look like thick chocolate milk.

In these muddy waters, my brother and I would play football with our friends, splashing through the charcos with a slippery, wet football until our mother would yell at us. She would swing open the front screen door and scream.

"¡Huercos cochinos! Get out of that charco! ¡Parecen marranos!"

It was in these charcos where we would find sapos. They were easy to locate because they made that loud, low croaking sound. And once we found them, they couldn't get away because they were slow and we were many. We were usually in a gang of four or five, and we'd surround the sapo and catch it. It was really something if one of us caught a sapo in the middle of its hop. Once we had captured a sapo, it would wiggle and squirm, but it was of no use. It would stop after a minute and just sit there without an expression.

I would make sure that the sapo was the size of my palm so I could ensure a good throw. Also, it was important that its legs and arms fell between my fingers. If we caught a sapo that was too small, we'd put it in a box for other uses. After catching a sapo that was just right, I would stand next to the tall palm tree in my neighbor's yard. I'd look up at the leaves of the tall palm tree. The outline of the leaves looked like curved blades against the cloudy sky. Then, with all my strength, I would throw that sapo.

"Eeeeee-loooooo," my brother and friends would say with glee and awe. That sapo would fly high, as high as the palm tree. It would reach its zenith and then stop for a second. In that second, my brother, my friends, and I would stand there looking up at the weightless sapo, its arms and legs stretched out as if it were going to fly away like a bird. But no. It would come down as fast as it went up. "¡Palo!" It would hit the damp ground; no blood, no screaming sounds like cats make when you throw them, and no expression on its gray-green face. It would just lie there—dead.

"Eeeeeee-loooooo! Ese sapo went high," they would say with amazement. We'd all laugh. "Let's go look for some more sapos!"

And so the day would be devoted to finding sapos and thinking of new ways to have fun with them. We'd play catch with sapos, we'd tie kite string around them and swing them like a sling, watching the poor sapos fly across our yard trailing a kite string. They would hit the ground, bounce, and lie motionless. We'd shoot them with BB guns. We'd sit there with our BB guns and watch the sapo and wait till it croaked. Its neck would get big with air and we'd take aim. One block from our house was Highway 107, and that highway was built for cars and sapos. We'd take them out to Highway 107 and place one in the middle of the double yellow lines. And if it managed to hop off the highway safely, we'd put it back in the middle of the double yellow lines.

One weekend my parents went to San Antonio to visit our tía and tío and left my brother and me with our older cousin, Berta. She was from Weslaco and was supposed to be real smart. Berta was nice and she could drive a car. Our parents left Friday afternoon, even though it was raining, and that night Berta let us stay up till midnight and watch TV. All night it rained, and through the sound of the rain we could hear the sapos croaking loud.

On Saturday mornings, our friends would get to our house around nine o'clock. When they did, we all had to go outside. We weren't allowed to play in the house because we always seemed to break something. Outside, the sky was still cloudy and dark. The ground was damp, and the charcos were full of muddy water and sapos. First, we played football in the charcos. Cousin Berta said it was bueno to play in the charcos, but we had to hose ourselves off outside before going in the house. It was fine with us, because then we could have a water fight. After playing football for a while, our attention turned to the sapos. We'd walk through the charcos with a box, looking for them. We caught a sapo for each person and went to the palm tree. What we didn't know was that Berta was watching us from the screen door. I was going to throw first since I could throw the highest, and inside I felt that maybe I could throw this sapo past the leaves of the palm tree. I took a couple of deep breaths and threw as hard as I could. I watched that sapo fly. Then we heard a scream.

"Eeeeeeee! ¿Qué están haciendo?" Berta came running out of the house. She let out a scream as the sapo flew straight up. The sapo reached its zenith just past the highest palm leaf. Berta's eyes were fixed on the wingless sapo. Like the others before, it came flying down as fast as it went up. ¡Palo! Its gray-green body hit the damp ground.

"What's wrong with you? You just killed that poor sapo." Berta said in an angry tone. My friends stood still, saying nothing. My brother looked at me.

I looked at Cousin Berta. "It's just a sapo!" I said.

Berta placed one hand on her hip and pointed at me with the other. With her finger pointed at me, she jabbed the air between us with each word.

"¡Ah, sí! Cómo te gustaría if I threw you up in the air and watched you die?" Berta said. "Look at that sapo! You just killed it, por nada!"

"No más son sapos," I said. "Mira, the charcos are full of them." I pointed to the ditches filled with muddy water. My brother and my friends were as confused as I was. They stood there looking at Cousin Berta, each with a sapo in his hand, ready to throw. Cousin Berta's eyes quickly scanned them, and she saw the remaining sapos surrounded by fingers. Sapos with no expressions, trapped in the hands of "huercos cochinos."

"Put those sapos back in the charco!" she said, pointing at the charco.

"Pero, Prima, they took a long time to catch," my brother said.

"¿Sabes por qué? Because they don't want to be caught and tortured," she said. "Ahora, put those sapos back in the charco right now!"

"All of them?" I asked.

"¡Sí, todos!" she said.

"Even the ones in the box?" I asked.

"What box?"

Orlando pointed to the box by the palm tree. It was the box with the small sapos. Cousin Berta immediately walked over to the box, and when she saw the small sapos sitting in the box, she bit her lower lip and looked like a dog growling.

"Put all these sapos, all of them, back in the charco!" Cousin Berta looked pretty mad, so we did what she said. Orlando was going to throw his sapo at the charco from where we were standing, but Cousin Berta didn't let him. We let all the sapos go back in the charco, and we turned the box of sapos over in the charco too. Sapos hopped and swam to their freedom.

After all the sapos were free, Cousin Berta made our friends go home and told my brother and me to get in the house. My brother and I spent the remainder of the afternoon watching TV, and for supper Berta made tacos. The kitchen had the warm aroma of corn tortillas and carne. At the center of the table was a bowl filled with lettuce and tomatoes, and on each plate were three hot, greasy tacos. Cousin Berta didn't look mad anymore and she was being nice to us.

Outside it was dark, and the cool, damp night air flowed through the kitchen screen door. Every now and then we could hear cars and eighteen-wheelers passing on Highway 107. The cars that passed in front of our house drove slowly, their tires breaking the rocks of the gravel road. Invisible dogs were barking at something they saw or smelled. But what we could hear the most were sapos croaking. The long, low moaning sounds were continuous. As if there were a choir of sapos singing, "Row, row, row your boat." Cousin Berta leaned back in her chair and looked at us. We were happy, my brother and I. Cousin Berta wasn't mad anymore, and our stomachs were full of tacos.

"Esos sapos are sure making a lot of noise tonight, aren't they?" she said. My brother and I looked at each other as if to say, "Where did that come from?"

"They always make noise," my brother said.

"Sí, pero, they don't always make that much noise," Cousin Berta said.

"Well, yeah, they're sapos. They're supposed to make noise. They don't do anything else," I said.

"No, sapos do more than just make noise."

"Bueno, they hop and swim and sometimes they pee on you," I said. My brother and I laughed, but my cousin Berta didn't laugh. She just looked at us with a small, scary grin.

"Do you know why I think those sapos are making so much noise? Because I think they're mad at both of you. And tonight, when you are sleeping, they're going to get inside this house and kill you!" she said in a very serious tone. My brother looked at me and I looked at him. We both started laughing.

"¡No, hombre, no! I'll give ese sapo un patazo!" I said. My brother followed my bold statement.

"¡No, que no!" We both laughed. Cousin Berta didn't laugh; she just looked at us with a small grin.

"Have you ever seen a sapo inside your house?" Berta asked. My brother and I were still laughing over the thought of a sapo trying to kill us. "You have, haven't you?" she continued.

"Yeah, we've seen a sapo in the house," my brother answered. "But it didn't try to kill us!" My brother continued laughing. Cousin Berta looked a little mad, but she didn't say anything; she just waited till we stopped laughing. Gradually our laughing became giggling, and then just a hee and a ha here and there.

"Remember that dead baby they found in Weslaco?" she asked.

We sat still trying to recall the exact events surrounding the famous dead baby. The Valley newspapers ran stories on the dead baby, and doctors tried to figure out how the baby died. But no one really knew.

"Do you know your tía Carmen's friend Lucía?" Berta asked. We knew Lucía very well. Tía Carmen and Lucía were good friends, and everybody in Weslaco would see Lucía to get cured. See, Lucía was a curandera and everyone respected her.

"When the parents found their baby in the crib not breathing, they called Lucía first," Berta said. "¿Y sabes qué? Lucía said she found a sapo in the room where the baby was sleeping, and she also found a yellow stain on the baby's clothes."

We knew what the yellow stain meant. Sapos would sometimes pee on you if you held them wrong, and the pee would get your clothes dirty.

"Lucía said the sapo killed that baby, and there was nothing anybody could do to bring that dead baby back!" Berta said. My brother and I looked at each other. We weren't laughing and my brother looked scared and I was scared.

"Un sapo could get in this house tonight and kill both of you just like that sapo killed that poor baby," Berta said. "It comes in your house hopping very quietly and walks through the house smelling the air. Smelling the charco water in your hair. Then, when the sapo finds your room, it squeezes underneath the door. It watches you sleep, then it jumps on your bed. It walks very slowly up toward your head. It gets on your chest and moves up to your neck."

Berta made body movements like the sapo would. She then put her hands out as if to grab us.

"It grabs your throat with its little hands." Berta's hands grasped the air in front of us. "At the end of each finger, sapos have small suction cups and they won't let go of your neck. It will choke you to death!"

Berta looked at us. Her dark brown eyes looked black, and she just kept on looking at us. I looked over at Roger, who was right next to me, my shoulder touching his shoulder. Roger looked at me and suddenly his eyes became big.

"But I didn't kill any sapos today!" Roger burst out. "David killed lots of them today, but I didn't kill any."

"¿Qué? I only killed one today, and yesterday you killed lots of sapos. And you're always killing baby sapos with bottle rockets and firecrackers," I said.

"¡Ya! It doesn't matter how many you killed," Berta said. "Ahora both of you go to bed. Ya es tarde."

We did as Cousin Berta said, and once we were in our room, Roger and I looked underneath our beds to see if any sapos were there. Nothing. We looked in the closet and in the trash can. Nothing. We felt a little better after having searched the room. But Roger was still nervous.

Outside the sapos were croaking, making low sounds that traveled through the window screens.

"They sound like they're right outside!" Roger said.

"Roger, they sound like that all the time."

I got up from my bed and closed the windows.

"Ya! Is that better now?" I said, as if I had only closed the window for his sake. Roger looked a little better, then his eyes saw the light. The light that squeezed underneath the door into our room.

"It can still get in here!" he said. "¡Mira!" Roger pointed to the thin light. He was right. Cousin Berta said that a sapo could get in a room by going under the door. Once again, I got up and turned on the bedroom light. I grabbed our big dictionary and the biggest encyclopedias. I stacked them against the foot of the door. They were heavy books, and I felt confident that no sapo could push those books aside. Roger and I slept well.

The next day my friends came over, and again we played football in the charcos. After a soaking game of football, Orlando picked up his BB gun and said, "Let's go shoot some sapos!" I looked at him and Roger looked at me.

"¡No, hombre, no! Let's shoot some gatos!" I said. And so we spent the rest of the day hunting cats.

El Cucuy

Roger and I were like other five- and six-year-old boys. We ran around yelling and screaming, chasing each other all day long like a dog chases his tail. We did this for no apparent reason, and if we weren't chasing each other, we were fighting or doing something equally loud. Our parents both worked so it was hard for our mother to keep the house clean and keep an eye on us. So we had maids.

In the Rio Grande Valley having a maid was not as expensive as one might think. Every maid who worked for our family was a Mexican national, and most didn't speak a word of English, which didn't bother us because we were also Mexican, except that we were born north of the border.

When we were growing up, we had maids that would quit working for us within weeks, sometimes days. We had five maids in all, and each one had different ways of trying to make us behave: mean stares, yelling, threats, bribes, begging, and the old standby, crying.

In the end they would give up, but not before telling our mother what they thought of Roger and me. They would say that we were traviesos, and one even thought we had the devil in us.

Cata, our last maid and the one who lived with us for more than six years, was very different from all the rest. Her approach to controlling us involved reaching deep into our psyche and tapping our innate fear. The fear of El Cucuy.

Cata was a small, slim woman. She had long black hair with lines of white running through it, but she mostly wore her hair in a bun so you couldn't tell how long it was, but it was long. She always wore a white Mexican dress and faded white chanclas. Even when it was cold outside she wore the same thing, but with a blue shawl around her small shoulders.

Her skin was darker than my father's and her eyes were a deep brown. She was probably the oldest maid we ever had, but it was hard to tell how old she was because Mexican women don't show their age. My abuelita never looked her age.

The first night we were left alone with Cata, we decided to test her out. Cata was in the kitchen cleaning up, and Roger and I were running in and out of the kitchen just to annoy her. She said something about time to go to bed, but her voice was drowned out by our shouts and yells.

Then Cata dropped some spoons and forks on the floor. The sound of the metal spoons and forks startled us, and we stopped running and looked at her. She looked scared.

"¡Oye! Did you hear that?" Her brown eyes slowly moved to the back door and then to us. All we could hear was the chatter of the television.

"I don't hear anything," I said.

"Neither do I," Roger said.

"What you heard was the television," I said.

"Yeah," Roger said.

Cata walked over to the television, turned it off, and looked at us. "I heard something scratching at the door. I think it's out there."

"There's nothing out there. It's just the wind," I said with confidence in my voice. "Look, I'll even open the door and show you nothing is out there."

Cata's eyes got big and she began shaking her hands. "No, no, don't do that. Because that's what it wants you to do so it can grab you."

"What, what's going to grab me?" I asked.

Cata paused for a moment and looked at us. "El Cucuy is out there. Not just one, but two. And they want to get both of you."

We both dropped our guard for a second, then I, being the oldest, spoke first. "There is no such thing as El Cucuy."

"Yeah, it's like Santa Claus. It's make-believe," Roger added.

Cata looked at us and nodded her head slowly. "Ah sí, El Cucuy vive. El Cucuy knows you two are baaaad little boys and traviesos and that's why El Cucuy is outside waiting to get you."

Roger looked a little worried, and I, too, was beginning to worry so I tried to reason El Cucuy away.

"El Cucuy is not real; my mother told me so," I said, though my mother had never said such a thing.

Cata raised her brow as if to say, ¡Ah sí! She placed her hands on her hips. "You believe in God, don't you?" Cata nodded.

Roger and I shrugged our shoulders and nodded. "Yeah."

"And God has angels, doesn't he?" We nodded yes again, following the motion of Cata's head.

"Bueno, now the devil has El Cucuy—not just one Cucuy, but lots of them. Every time a new soul enters the world, God gives that soul, boy or girl, and angel to protect them from all the evil in the world. If you are good, your angel helps you and protects you," Cata said with a small smile, but her smile faded as she proceeded. "But the devil is never far."

"Bueno, the devil makes sure that for every new soul in the world there is a Cucuy, and El Cucuy feeds off you. The meaner you are, the stronger El Cucuy gets, and then it comes to get you."

Roger and I were terrified. All I could hear was dogs barking down the street. Cata was smart. She knew she had us scared, but she wasn't finished yet.

"Do you know why those dogs are barking?" Cata asked.

Roger and I shook our heads.

"They know what Cucuys smell like, and they're afraid because they know Cucuys like to eat dogs. Sometimes when a dog is missing, you think it's lost. It's not lost; it's because a Cucuy was hungry and ate it, and they eat cats too. Have you ever seen a Cucuy?" We hadn't and Cata knew it.

"They say El Cucuy is only as tall as you are, but they can be very strong. They have long claws on their hands and feet, and when they walk on floors or streets, their claws click and scratch. They can climb trees and the sides of houses very easily. They have small, sharp, pointed teeth, and saliva is always falling out of their mouths, just like with dogs or cows. They have long, pointed ears and can hear you whisper. They can hear you whisper bad, mean things. Some have red eyes and some have yellow eyes, and they look like cat eyes. They know what you smell like just like your dog knows. You can't hide from El Cucuy, but if you are good, he stays away."

Roger and I said nothing, and I didn't hear the dogs barking anymore. I looked into Cata's eyes and wasn't sure if they were brown or yellow. Roger and I were terrified.

I looked at the faded Palm Sunday cross hanging over our front door. And I looked at the living room wall where a painted picture of our Lord Jesus Christ hung. It was an image of Christ wearing a crown of thorns. Blood dripped down the side of his forehead, and his eyes looked up to Heaven. I looked at Roger, and he looked like he was about to cry.

"If we ask God to forgive us and if we are good, do you think El Cucuy will stay away?" I asked in a humble tone.

"I don't know. Only God knows. Now it's time to go to bed, and don't forget to brush your teeth."

We brushed our teeth and went to bed and prayed El Cucuy would eat Cata and not us.

Tina La Tinaca

Tina stood patiently in line. The wait gave her time to decide what she wanted from the menu board. Tina loved hot dogs with plenty of chile con carne and cheese.

The football stadium was filling up for the game between the Edcouch-Elsa Fighting Yellow Jackets and the Mercedes Tigers. The stadium lights gave the football field a bright, fresh green color, almost glossy, and the white lines and numbers appeared to have depth. In Edcouch-Elsa, everyone went to the football games and cheered after every play.

Tina was excited about the game and she was proud of her new shirt, a gray short-sleeved cotton T-shirt with the words "Edcouch-Elsa Fighting Yellow Jackets" printed on it in black and gold letters. The letters were stretched and distorted across her breasts and stomach because the shirt was too snug, but large was the largest size they had. Tina ordered three hot dogs, a large popcorn, two large sodas, and a pickle for her son, Héctor. She walked slowly toward the bleachers, making sure not to drop her tray of snacks.

In one section of the stands a group of boys sat together ridiculing every person walking by. The girls were judged and then given a score between one and ten, one being "muy fea" and ten being "muy bonita." When they saw Tina walking by in her new T-shirt, one of the boys was quick with a comment.

"Esa parece como el tinaco de Edcouch," he said. The boys laughed. From that first laugh, people in town referred to Tina as

"Tina la Tinaca." Tina didn't know she looked like a water tower in her new gray T-shirt. She just kept walking, looking for Héctor. Héctor kept an eye out for his mother, and as soon as he saw her, he waved his arms to get her attention. Once seated, they enjoyed the game.

Tina loved Héctor. She was grateful to God for the gift he had sent her. Héctor came to her through her brother, Rubén. Rubén was a borracho. His wife of three years had left him and Héctor, and he left Héctor with Tina. Rubén never came back, and so Héctor became Tina's son. Héctor didn't remember his father or mother very well, but he knew Tina and soon considered her his mother.

Tina was a happy person. She enjoyed her job at the health clinic, filing papers all day and answering the phone. She kept her files as neat as she kept her house. It was a nice blue frame house with a clean yard and a colorful bed of flowers. She manicured her flowers weekly, and the man next door, Paco, mowed her lawn every couple of weeks for five dollars.

The inside of her house was as clean as her yard. On top of the television she had photographs of Héctor taken through the years and photos of them together taken at the Argüelles department store in Elsa. Her kitchen, too, was clean. Every morning she made breakfast for Héctor and herself. The kitchen would fill with the warm aroma of papas con huevos or chorizo con huevos, but no matter what they ate, there were always hot tortillas de harina. They would eat their breakfast and somehow Tina always managed to clean the kitchen before going to work.

Héctor's room was no different from the rest of the house. When Héctor left for school in the morning, his room would be a mess, but by the time he came home he would find it clean. His room would not only be clean but in order. His shirts were all on hangers and his shoes paired up in a straight row.

Tina had decided that in the summer she would take Héctor to Houston. Héctor liked watching the Houston Astros baseball team on television, and Tina had always wanted to visit the Astroworld amusement park. Something for each of us, she thought.

Héctor was excited about visiting Astroworld and watching the Astros play in the Astrodome. He thought that maybe he should take his glove in case one of the players hit a foul ball or even a home run in his direction. He imagined catching that wild ball and everybody in the Valley seeing him catch it on KRIO-TV, channel 8, "home of the Houston Astros."

When he told his friends he was going to Astroworld and was going to watch the Astros play, most were impressed, but Lupe was a little jealous.

"How are you going to Houston?" Lupe asked. Héctor said his mother was taking him.

"She's not your mother," Lupe said. "Tina is your tía!" Héctor knew this was true, but Tina was still his mother.

"She's my mother!" Héctor repeated furiously.

"Tina is your tía! Your father was a drunk and left you with Tina. And your real mother left you too!" Lupe said.

Héctor followed his emotions and charged Lupe. Both fell to the ground swinging and kicking. Héctor's glasses flew off his face. Héctor grabbed Lupe's shirt and tore it. Lupe managed to hit Héctor in the face but didn't leave any marks. Both were pulled apart by their friends, but Héctor was still angry.

"¿Por qué te enojas? ¡Es la verdad! ¡Tina la Tinaca es tu tía!" Lupe said.

The boys began to laugh. It was the first time Héctor had heard the secret nickname everyone in town knew. Héctor felt like crying. He grabbed his broken glasses off the ground and began walking home. One of the boys called out to him to come back but another quickly said to let him go.

Héctor told his mother he broke his glasses playing football. Tina believed him. Héctor now began spending most of his time at home, but it didn't bother him. He and Tina would go to church together, and every now and then they'd drive to McAllen to see a movie.

Within a few months Tina managed to save the money needed for the trip to Houston. She bought a Texas road map, and together they plotted their route. She laid out the map on the kitchen table but was confused by all the curved lines. She had never taken a trip by herself and knew she had to be confident in front of Héctor. With her stubby right index finger she pointed to the small dot on the map that represented Edcouch. "De aquí we want to go here." Her stubby left index finger landed on the big word "Houston."

While studying the map, Héctor began to worry that maybe they couldn't make the trip, but after seeing that it took only two major roads, Highway 77 and Interstate 59, to get there, he began to feel better. They would take Highway 77 through Raymondville, the Sarita checkpoint, Kingsville, and Robstown. In Victoria they would hop onto Interstate 59, which was a straight drive to Houston. They decided to take a small ice chest filled with sodas, cookies, tacos, and pan dulce.

On Friday morning Tina and Héctor left Edcouch. It was a comfortable drive because Tina's Chevrolet Impala had an air conditioner that cooled well. As they drove they ate the snacks they had brought. Tina spun the dial on the radio looking for a station she and Héctor both liked.

By late afternoon Tina and Héctor arrived in Houston. Neither could believe the number of cars and how big the roads were. Some roads were four lanes and others were six lanes wide. Héctor even saw jets and helicopters flying in the sky, something he had never seen in Edcouch.

It was some time before they found a motel. The clerk at the counter said that Astroworld and the Astrodome could be seen from the second floor, so Tina asked for a room up there. The clerk was right. They could see the Astrodome's silver roof and the colorful neon lights of Astroworld. They both took a shower and later watched TV, flipping through the many channels before going to sleep. In the darkness of the strange motel walls, Tina spoke to Héctor. "Mijo, are you having a good time?"

"Sí, Amá, this is the best time I have ever had in my whole life!"

On Saturday morning Astroworld opened at nine o'clock, and they arrived with tickets in hand. They rode all the rides, and to Tina's surprise, she could fit in every seat. She even saw several people who were bigger than she. Clearly, Tina was not as fat as she thought.

Tina saw a photo booth that had a cut-out, life-size picture of one of the roller coaster rides. Seated behind the picture, Tina and Héctor raised their arms as if on a roller coaster. They began to laugh. The photograph was ready in minutes, and they bought a blue frame with the words "Astroworld" in red at the top. Both were pleased with the photograph.

That night they watched fireworks blaze in the sky. They were the same type as those Héctor had seen on television at the beginning of each Walt Disney movie. The park closed at eleven o'clock, and they stayed until the last blaze.

The next day they got up early because they were excited about seeing the Astrodome. The baseball game started at one o'clock, but they were there by noon.

They walked around looking for their section. Héctor had seen the Astrodome on television dozens of times and was thrilled about watching a real, professional baseball game.

Tina found the concession stand and was pleased to see hot dogs on the menu board. The sodas came in plastic cups that had "Astrodome" and "Houston Astros" printed on them. This made Héctor very happy.

After the game they walked around in the parking lot of the Astrodome, searching for their car. Héctor saw their car first and began to run, weaving in and out between parked cars. Then he ran around a parked van and into the path of a slow-moving white truck. Héctor's eyes focused on the brightness of the setting Sunday sun reflected off the chrome grill of the truck. Tina heard the short screech of the tires and the hollow metal sound the truck made when Héctor's body hit the hood.

Tina was in shock, and all she could say was, "Mijo, mijo." She tried to get Héctor to talk. "Mijo, mijo!" she cried out, but not a sound came from Héctor's limp body. Within minutes an ambulance drove up. Two men jumped out. One man attended to Héctor; the other tried to talk to Tina. "Ma'am, is this your son?" he asked. "Ma'am, is this your son?" Tina could hear nothing; everything became twisted. She looked around and saw people surrounding her and the lights from the ambulance flashing blue and red. The ambulance drivers got another stretcher and laid Tina down on it.

Minutes later Tina was in a police car following the ambulance. The police officer was Mexican American but didn't speak Spanish. He asked Tina questions as they drove. "Where are you from? Where? Do you have any family here in Houston? Where is your car?" Tina could hear the questions, but her answers were slow. "I'm from Edcouch. It's in the Valley. No. I left the car in the parking lot." The police officer assured her everything was going to be OK, but Tina didn't feel well—she was scared and confused.

At the hospital Tina was met by a social worker. She was a white woman who spoke Spanish. "Yo hablo español," she said. She asked the same questions as the police officer, then asked if Tina had any family in the Valley, and what her religion was. Tina told her she had a brother, Rubén, but hadn't seen him in six years, and she belonged to the St. Theresa Catholic Church in Edcouch. The social worker had a police officer look up the town judge of Edcouch, thinking maybe he could help.

Judge Gómez was a good man, and when he received the call from the social worker, he was quick to offer whatever help Tina needed. She told Judge Gómez that Héctor was not going to make it because he had suffered too much brain damage. She also told the judge that he would receive a call as soon as Héctor died, and that Tina was in no condition to drive. "No problem," said the judge. "I'll have a couple of my police officers go up there and drive Tina back down."

Judge Gómez was worried about Tina. "Pobrecita," he said to himself. He knew how she felt about Héctor. The judge was the one who had signed the papers allowing Tina to become Héctor's legal guardian. He remembered how happy she had been when he signed the legal documents. "Gracias, muchas gracias, Judge Gómez. Que Dios lo bendiga," she had said.

Tina sat in the waiting room alone. She kept getting up and pacing the small room, rubbing her hands as she prayed in Spanish. The social worker entered the room with a priest and the doctor. The priest was Mexican American, and his skin was dark like Tina's. The doctor was a white man; he was lean, tall, and wore glasses.

"Tina, this is Father Víctor Sánchez and this is Doctor Crenshaw; they want to talk to you about Héctor," she said. Tina placed her hands in Father Víctor's hands and began to cry. She asked the priest to pray for Héctor, to pray that he'd be fine. The doctor was uncomfortable. He didn't understand Spanish, and he did not like being the messenger of death.

They all sat down on the waiting room sofas, and the doctor described to Tina how severe Héctor's head injuries were. He told her that Héctor would die in the next twenty-four hours, and that he had done the best he could, but it was all in God's hands.

Tina felt weak; the priest put his arms around her and said it was time to read the last rites to Héctor to prepare his soul for God's kingdom. He gave her a rosary to hold, and together they walked down the hall of the intensive care wing, passing rooms that held other patients living off machines. Héctors bed was surrounded by others like him, people dying, connected to beeping and hissing machines.

The priest began his prayers, while Tina held Héctor's cold little hand. Tina couldn't believe it was Héctor. His head was swollen and his face was blue, his dark brown eyes shut tight by the swelling. He didn't look like Héctor; she almost didn't accept it was Héctor until she looked at his hands. It was his hand she held, it was his body, and it was Héctor who was dying. How she hoped this was all some terrible dream, but she could feel the cold air of the wing of the dying.

Judge Gómez called his two police officers, Julio and Joel Barco. They were brothers who had learned how to be policemen by watching television and movies. Judge Gómez wondered if they would ever get an offer to work in some other town. When the judge told them about Tina, one of them interrupted him. "You mean Tina la Tinaca?"

"No!" the judge snapped angrily. "I mean Tina." The Barcos stuffed their hands in their pockets and said nothing.

"Now listen," the judge said. "Héctor, Tina's son, has been involved in a car accident, and the doctors say he is not going to make it. I want both of you to drive up to Houston and bring Tina back, and if possible, the boy's body. The social worker up there says Tina is in no condition to drive. Understand?"

Both men nodded.

"Now, right now it's eight o'clock, and I want you two to take the city ambulance to bring back Héctor's body. You may want to put some bags of ice in the ambulance on the way back so the boy's body will stay cold." The judge thought for a moment. "Also, one of you will have to drive Tina back down in her car."

"Julio will drive her back down," Joel said.

"¿Qué? You're going to," Julio was quick to reply.

"No, hombre. Last time . . ." Joel was about to answer, but was cut off by the judge.

"I don't care who drives what. Just get it done! And when you get to Houston, call me." Thinking to himself, the judge truly wished he could get some other officers.

Julio and Joel bought some snacks and cold beer for the trip. They drove the same route Tina and Héctor had driven two days earlier. On the way up they flipped a coin to see who would drive the ambulance and who would drive with Tina. Joel lost.

At four in the morning Judge Gómez received the call that Héctor had died. The judge talked to Tina and told her everything was going to be fine. "Tina, I'm sorry to hear about Héctor, but listen, the Barcos are on their way up there to bring you and Héctor back home. So don't worry about the trip, ¿bueno?" The judge also spoke to the social worker and explained that the Barcos were on their way, and that they had been instructed to bring Tina and Héctor back to Edcouch.

When they arrived in Houston, Julio and Joel drove around for an hour looking for the hospital. After a few wrong exits and many WRONG WAY and NO U-TURN signs, they managed to find it. The social worker greeted them in the emergency room. "Bueno, buenos días," she said.

"Morning. I'm Joel Barco and this is my partner Julio Barco; we're here to pick up Miss Tina Guzmán and her son." Joel extended his hand. She shook his hand, then she shook Julio's hand.

"Yes, I'm Banford Wilson. I spoke to Judge Gómez just a couple of hours ago. He wants you to call him. Are you two brothers or something?"

"Yes, we're brothers," Julio said. "Where is Miss Guzmán, Miss Wilson?"

"She's in the waiting room; she hasn't slept all night, poor woman."

Tina sat on a chair in the waiting room unaware of the people around her. When she saw the Barcos walk in, people she knew, people like her, she began to cry.

"Julio, Joel, gracias a Dios que llegaron," she said in a breaking voice, her eyes watering. "Se murió mi hijo." Julio extended his arms to hug and console her, but it was difficult for him to express his emotions. Her body shook in his arms, and he looked over at Joel, who shrugged his shoulders, not knowing what he should do. Tina didn't notice. She was relieved to have someone she knew there in such a strange place where pain had become part of the walls and death greeted one at the door.

"Tina, don't worry. We're going to take you and Héctor back home. Bueno," Julio said. "Ya saben el judge y el padre." Julio was trying to ease her pain, but he knew that he was not the best at this sort of thing.

"Sí, Tina, everything will be fine. Joel will drive you home and Héctor will ride with me," Julio said. "We brought the city ambulance so we could take the body—I mean Héctor—back home." Tina nodded her head.

Arrangements were made with the hospital to allow the Barcos to take the body from the morgue, and Tina signed the necessary papers. Before getting the body, the Barcos drove Tina to the Astrodome to pick up her car, then to the motel to gather her belongings. In the motel room, Tina felt weak.

Joel tried to comfort her. "Tina, we have to get back home soon so you can talk to the priest, ¿bueno?" he said. Tina looked at the carpet, the television, and the strange multicolored striped walls. "The best time I ever had in my whole life," she heard Héctor's voice echo in the room.

The drive back was difficult for Joel. He and Tina rode in silence. Tina kept looking at the ambulance. At times they would fall behind a good distance, catch up, then fall behind again. They couldn't stay with the ambulance very long because Julio drove too fast.

When they arrived in Edcouch, they went directly to the Stillman Funeral Home so Tina could make arrangements with Mr. Stillman. Judge Gómez and the priest met Tina at the funeral home, and she cried when she saw them.

The women of the church led a beautiful rosary. Our Fathers and Hail Marys were repeated with sincerity as Tina held tightly onto her rosary. She tried not to think of what was happening by focusing on the glossy black beads, one by one.

The funeral was sad. People thought more about Tina than Héctor. "What is she going to do now?" they said. "Pobrecita."

The months after Héctor's death were not easy for Tina. She didn't talk to her co-workers as much as before, and she slowly began gaining more weight. She stopped wearing slacks and started wearing house dresses. She began calling in sick to work, sometimes taking two days off only to sit in her house and do nothing. Finally she quit. Tina had some money in savings and her house was paid for, so she figured she could go without working for a few months, maybe even a year.

People didn't see much of Tina anymore. She didn't go to the football games, nor did she attend church. The outside of her house began looking shabby. She didn't tend her flowers anymore, although Paco still mowed her lawn. A woman named Rosa began buying groceries for Tina. Tina would give Rosa two checks, one for ten dollars and the other for the groceries. Now Tina could stay in her house all the time and she did.

Tina did come out for the Easter Sunday mass, but she went to the early mass to avoid seeing people. She put on a black dress and a black veil to cover her face, and she took her rosary, the one with the black beads she knew so well.

Most people at church did not recognize Tina, and those who did were shocked. Tina had gained so much weight and her hair had turned a dark gray. Her eyes were sad eyes, not the eyes one should have on the day Christ rose from the dead. The parishioners looked colorful in their Easter Sunday clothes. The men were dressed in clean, pressed suits, and the women wore bright flowery-print dresses, but Tina was dressed in black. She was still in mourning. All through the mass Tina could see Héctor's casket at the altar, and she cried quiet tears.

Tina was not seen again for many weeks. On the first anniversary of Héctor's death Tina spent most of the day in church. She prayed the rosary, then she just sat in the pew. When the priest walked in and passed by her, he did not know who she was at first, but then, after looking back, he realized it was Tina. She had gained more weight, and her year or mourning had aged her. He thought maybe he should talk to her, but what could he say to ease her pain? He had seen people mourn like this before. That night he prayed for Tina.

Rosa hadn't spoken to Tina in over a week, so she called her to see if she needed any groceries, which would give her an excuse to use the car to see a special friend. There was no answer at Tina's house. Rosa called again that night, and again there was no answer. The next day Rosa walked from her house to Tina's.

Rosa saw Tina's car in the driveway and on reaching the door could smell a stench in the air. Rosa thought, What if Tina is dead? But that only happened on television. She knocked and called out, "Tina, soy yo, Rosa. ¿Tina?" No response. Again she called out. She slowly opened the front door and the smell overwhelmed her. Rosa gagged a little and called out, "Tina, Tina, soy yo, Rosa." Rosa began to worry. The house was warm, almost hot, because all the windows and doors were closed. There was trash everywhere. Empty cans and bottles littered the living room. The walls and the floors of the hall were streaked with brown stains, and dirty clothes lay in small piles in the hall and in the living room. Rosa was sick to her stomach from the smell of urine and waste.

She called out as she walked down the hall, knowing she would not get an answer. She passed the bathroom, which smelled as bad as the rest of the house. The next door on the right was Tina's room. She opened the door but could not get it to open all the way. Something was blocking the door. Rosa looked in and could see Tina's body lying face down parallel to the door. Tina's leg was blocking the door. "Tina, Tina," she said, but she knew the poor woman was probably dead. Rosa called the police from Tina's house and told them that she thought Tina was dead, but that they had better send an ambulance just in case she wasn't.

Julio was on duty when the call came in. He drove through the dirt street fast, kicking up dust and rocks. Not because he was concerned about Tina, but because he liked driving fast and watching the dust he left behind. Rosa stood outside the house waiting when Julio drove up. He stepped out of the car slowly, adjusting his belt and dark sunglasses.

"¿Qué pasa, Rosa?" he asked.

"I'm the one who called. I think Tina is dead," she said.

"Is she inside the house?"

"Sí, she's in her room. I can show you," she said.

On entering the house Julio was hit by the smell. "Oye, apesta a mea'os," he said.

"Yeah, it's real bad," Rosa said.

Julio couldn't believe what a mess the house was. Only houses that had been abandoned for months looked like this; kids would trash the house and sometimes urinate on the walls and floors.

"Man, what the hell happened here?" he asked as they walked down the short hall to Tina's room.

"You can't open the door all the way. Her leg is in the way," Rosa said. Julio pushed on the door until he could squeeze his way into the room. Tina's room was no different from the rest of the house. He looked down at her large body. Her gray hair was stiff and looked like wire. In fact, Tina didn't look real at all but more like a bloated mannequin. Just then, he heard one of the ambulance drivers calling out. "Julio is in here," Rosa said.

Johnny and Juan walked in with their first-aid kit. "Hey, Rosa. Where is she?" Johnny asked.

"She's in there with Julio. I think she's dead."

Johnny and Juan looked into the room.

"Come in here and help me move her away from the door," Julio said. The three men pulled Tina away from the door and turned her over. Juan felt for a pulse, though he knew she was dead.

Juan looked up at Julio and Johnny. "Está muerta," he said. "We better call the judge so he can pronounce her dead."

By now people were gathering outside. Some of the neighborhood kids were looking through the windows. Julio had to chase them away. He told the people to stay off the property. Julio called the judge from Tina's house and explained the situation. Minutes later the judge drove up and found a small crowd of people wondering what was going on. He nodded to some of them and walked inside. Seeing Tina lying on the floor stopped him for a few seconds. Tina's rosary hung to one side, and dark circles shadowed her eyelids. He looked over at Johnny and Juan.

"What did you men find?" he asked.

"She has no pulse, Judge," Juan said. "I checked. She's dead."

The judge pronounced Tina dead without question.

"Get her down to Stillman Funeral Home and don't let people see her body," the judge said. The judge left, and the three men began to move things out of the way so they could move Tina's body.

Juan drove the ambulance closer to the front door of the house so they could put Tina's body in. He and Johnny brought down a stretcher, but she didn't fit on it because it was too narrow. Then they tried to roll her body into a sheet to drag her out. The three men struggled to move her body out of the room, but only Tina's legs made it through the door.

"Esta vieja parece como un tinaco now. And all this dead weight," Julio said. "¿Sabes qué? Let me call the fire department. Some of the guys are there and they can help us get her out."

The Edcouch fire truck drove up along with the rescue unit. They pulled up to the house without sirens but with their emergency lights on. By now more people had gathered around Tina's house, asking questions.

The four firemen talked with Julio, Johnny, and Juan about how they could get Tina out of the house. They couldn't get her out through the windows because the windows were too high and too small, and she didn't fit through her own bedroom door.

One of the firemen who came with the rescue unit looked at Tina, then at the bedroom door. "Wait, any of you ever see that movie *Animal House*? You know, the one with John Belushi?" the fireman asked. Another fireman nodded, and Julio said yeah.

"Well, remember when the horse died in that office? Remember? They had to cut up the horse to get it out of the office. Well, same here, except it would be like cutting up a cow!" All the men laughed and nodded on hearing such a good, timely joke.

"Hey," the other fireman from the rescue unit spoke up. "We have a chain saw in the rescue van, and we could cut the door frame so we can get the body out." The men thought for a second or two.

"Yeah, man, it could work," Julio said. With that the men began to discuss where to cut the door frame and how much so they could get the body out. One of the firemen went out to the rescue van to get the chain saw. When the people saw this, they became really curious.

"Oye, ¿qué van a hacer con eso?" The fireman answered, "Nada."

The men marked where to cut, and the gas-powered chain saw was turned on. The saw could easily be heard in the street, and people looked at each other, not sure what to think.

Tina's body was moved two feet away from the door, and one of the men cut through the frame and wall. Dust and chips of wood and paint spewed from the wall, slowly covering up Tina's dress and body. When the chain saw began cutting through the sheetrock, a fine white dust settled over her body, enveloping it in a cloud of powder.

The men cut the door frame on both sides until they knew that Tina could be lifted or dragged out. They cursed as they pulled and dragged her body down the short hall, all the while complaining about the smell coming from Tina's heavy dead body. When they reached the front door, the found that Tina's body would not fit through the door. Again the chain saw was started.

People could see Tina's body just inside the doorway. Her feet were bare, and her brown legs and arms were covered with white dust. Again the chain saw threw dust into the air. Tina's house again slowly covered up her body.

Finally the men were able to get Tina out and heaved her into the ambulance. The people could see that the men were not gentle with Tina's body, but she was dead and they could tell she was heavy. The ambulance driver turned on the lights and drove away through the dirt streets.

The next night the Stillman Funeral Home held a closed-casket ceremony for Tina. Tina's supervisor from work wanted to say a few words, but Judge Gómez felt he should be the one to say something. The pews filled up with the townspeople, most of whom were not sure why they were there. The judge was not sure what he was going to say. He stood there and looked at the people, who were wondering what he was going to say.

"Everyone here knew Tina. She was a good woman who liked going to football games and church bingos. She was just like all of us here. Tina also had a son, Héctor, and like all of us here who have hijos and hijas . . . well, we love our kids, eh? When Tina came to me to adopt Héctor, she was pretty nervous, and when I signed the papers making her Héctor's legal guardian she was very happy.

"I know Tina is happy now because she is with Héctor. That is why she died, to be with him. None of us wants to be alone in this world or up there in Heaven, even though there are angels and God. I'm glad you came tonight. Let's pray for Tina and Héctor to be happy." Judge Gómez wasn't sure if what he had said was good or not, but some people cried nonetheless.

The funeral was held the next morning because the Valley sun would get very hot in the afternoon. Tina was buried next to Héctor. The judge attended the funeral, as well as Rosa and a couple of Tina's former co-workers. As Tina as lowered into the ground, no tears were shed.

At Tina's house Julio and Joel walked around making a list of the valuables. Judge Gómez wanted to know what could be salvaged and given to the church. Joel couldn't believe it smelled as bad as Julio had described it. Empty tin cans, dirty clothes, tissue papers, and cans of furniture polish were scattered throughout the house. Julio picked up one of the cans of polish and noticed it was empty. He picked up another and it too was empty. He found another and that was also empty. They were all empty. With all these empty cans of furniture polish you could think her furniture would be clean, he thought to himself.

"Man, this woman lived like a pig. Look at all this," Julio said.

"There was something wrong with her. I mean, it must have been because her kid died or something," Joel said.

"That doesn't mean you should turn into a pig or at least not as big as one," said Julio.

"Come on, man. The poor woman is dead."

"You didn't have to get her fat, dead body out of here," Julio said. "I mean, look, man, we had to cut down half the door to get her out. This woman was crazy. I mean, look at this house. Parece como una casa de marranos. She didn't care about anything. You would think she might at least clean the kitchen or her own bedroom, man."

Joel nodded. Walking down the hall past Tina's bedroom, he came to a locked door. He turned the knob a few times and pushed, but the door wouldn't open.

"Hey, Julio. This door is locked. What do you think?" Joel said.

"I don't know, man. It's probably full of dead pigs or something," he laughed. "You open it and you clean it." Together they broke the door open.

It was Héctor's room. The brothers stood in the center of the room. Héctor's bed was made with straight, folded edges. Julio opened the closet door, and there were Héctor's clothes hanging neatly on hangers. His shoes were paired up and in a straight row. No dust on his shoes. On the wall were posters of the Houston Astros baseball team and a black-and-gold Edcouch-Elsa High School pennant. Against the wall by the window was Héctor's dresser, looking shiny and new. On the dresser was a photograph in a blue frame.

It was the photograph of Tina and Héctor at Astroworld, their arms in the air as if on a roller coaster, laughing.

The Barcos didn't say a word for a few seconds. Then Julio looked over at Joel.

"Know why this room is so clean?"

Joel shook his head slowly.

"Because the door was locked. If Tina la Tinaca had gotten in here, it would be a mess, too."

Lucia's Last Curse

Vicente couldn't run fast enough. She was gaining on him. This was the third night in a row that this woman had chased him. He was scared because he couldn't wake up. He would look back at her as he ran. He could see her face clearly. Her body moved with the cold wind that penetrated his body. With her arms extended and open hand, she grabbed his shoulder. The touch of her clammy skin would jerk his body so violently that he'd finally escape by waking up in a cold sweat.

Eddie came into Vicente's room.

"You all right?" he asked.

"Yeah, I'm OK," Vicente said.

"Yeah? Well, you're also making crazy chicken sounds. Did you have another one of those bad dreams?"

Vicente slowly shook his head and let out a quiet sigh. His roommate and friend of fifteen years had never seen him look so sick. Eddie shook his head and shrugged his shoulders.

"What did the alcoholic doctor at the student health clinic say?"

Vicente coughed a bit and let out a weak laugh. "He gave me a shot and told me to rest."

"Hey, I better call your mom," Eddie said. "You really don't look good. I think you better go to the hospital. It's that or go to a veterinarian so they can put you to sleep."

"*Pffft*, I can't even afford a vet," Vicente said.

"Yeah, well, get some rest. I'll call your mom and get your homework from the profs, OK?"

Vicente nodded slowly and pulled the covers up above his shoulders.

Eddie called Vicente's mother in Corpus Christi to tell her how sick Vicente was. She was a worrier, and Eddie did his best to make it sound as if Vicente wasn't that sick, but sick enough.

"Has he been to the doctor?" she asked.

"Yes, but he's still sick and it's been like this for almost a week."

"Eddie, can you please bring him home tonight?" she asked. "And I'll take care of him, ¿bueno?"

"Sure, Mrs. Rodríguez, whatever I can do."

Mrs. Rodríguez hung up the phone and thought for a few moments. Her poor son was always getting sick, and everything happened to him. She thought that maybe what Vicente needed was a curandera, but there weren't any good ones in Corpus Christi. She decided to call her sister Viola, in the Rio Grande Valley. Viola always knew what to do.

Viola listened to her sister, and when she heard the idea of asking a curandera for help, she knew exactly whom to ask. Viola knew a young woman, Ana, who attended Pan American University and helped her around the house. Ana's mother was the best curandera in the Valley. Viola told her sister that she would ask Ana if her mother would be willing to drive to Corpus to cure Vicente.

Later that afternoon, when Ana came to the house, Viola told her how sick Vicente was and asked if her mother would be nice enough to go up to Corpus and see if she could cure him. Ana had worked for Viola for over a year and had met Vicente a few times. She was only two years older than Vicente, and she liked him and felt a strong sense of family when they were together. So she readily agreed to ask her mother.

Lucía was a woman whom many of the old people in the Valley feared. She had strong healing powers, and some said she also practiced *negro* when she was younger. Lucía lived just outside of Hargill, a small town twenty miles from Edinburg. Nobody lived around her because the farmers said the land around her house was not good for growing anything but bruja plants.

But that was then, and now all the work she did was good. Every night she prayed to the Virgin Mary for the power to heal. Deep in her soul, she wanted to be forgiven for her evil past.

When Lucía heard of Vicente's illness, she saw it as one more good deed to counter the evil deeds of her past. Her daughter said it would involve a trip to Corpus Christi, but Lucía felt a trip would be nice. And besides, Viola was good to Ana and always paid her on time.

Mrs. Rodríguez was happy to hear that Viola had found a curandera so quickly, and she began to clean the house for her guests. She knew that Lucía was in her early sixties and expected that Viola and Lucía would probably spend the night.

Eddie could see that Vicente was having a difficult time keeping his head up. Vicente had not had a decent night's sleep since he had gotten sick, and the bad dreams made it only worse.

"Hang in there, man, we're almost home," Eddie said.

Vicente just nodded his head slowly. By six o'clock they arrived in Corpus Christi.

Mrs. Rodríguez came out and helped Eddie bring Vicente into the house. Vicente's body had given in to the illness, leaving him no strength to walk. He was glad to be home, a place where he knew he would be loved and cared for.

That night Mrs. Rodríguez made soup and fed her son, one spoonful at a time. She put a cool, wet towel on his head to keep his fever down and stayed with him until he fell asleep.

Ana and her mother arrived in Edcouch at noon. Viola had made some food for the women. They ate lunch and talked about how much the Valley had grown. Viola noticed that Lucía had brought a small black suitcase and figured it had to be some overnight clothes.

Viola was a little nervous; she felt a strange energy coming from Lucía. She felt as if the priest were visiting, but that Lucía was different and there were others with Lucía, looking and walking in the house.

By one o'clock, Viola and Lucía were on their way to Corpus Christi. Both women said a small prayer before leaving. Lucía mumbled a few extra words in Spanish that Viola couldn't make out. It was a cool November day in southern Texas with blue skies and feather clouds riding the high, cold wind streams. Lucía gathered her black shawl around her. "It's going to be a cold winter," she said softly to herself.

During the drive Lucía asked simple questions, asking where Viola was from and where her mother was from. Viola said that she was from San Benito, but her mother was from San Marcos, and that's where both her parents now lived.

"Ah, how long have they lived in San Marcos?" Lucía asked.

"Most of their lives. They only lived in San Benito a couple of years," Viola answered. Lucía nodded.

The rest of the drive was the same; every now and then another simple question, and Lucía would nod her head.

Mrs. Rodríguez was glad to see her sister and gave her a hug. Viola introduced Lucía to her sister, who extended her hand with a warm smile.

"Gracias a Dios que veniste, señora Lucía," she said.

Lucía nodded. "I hope with God's help I can heal your son, Mrs. Rodríguez."

Mrs. Rodríguez smiled. "Please, Señora Lucía, you can call me Becky."

The women made their way into the house. Lucía carried her black suitcase, and as she entered the house made the sign of the cross and mumbled some words in Spanish.

Vicente could hear the women's voices through the wall. He could make out his tía's voice but couldn't recognize the third. Lucía sat down on the sofa and looked around the living room. Mrs. Rodríguez asked if she wanted anything to drink or eat. Lucía asked for a glass of water, Mrs. Rodríguez walked into the kitchen. "Viola tells me you lived in San Benito for two years," Lucía said.

"Yes, yes, we lived in San Benito for a little bit. Then I got married and moved here to Corpus Christi, and Viola also got married and moved to Edcouch," Mrs. Rodríguez said.

"¿Y tu esposo es de San Benito?" Lucía asked. "No, he's from Corpus Christi, but he lived with his grandmother in San Benito for a while," Mrs. Rodríguez said. "We got married here in Corpus and stayed here."

Lucía nodded and let her eyes casually search the room for photos of Mrs. Rodríguez's husband.

"Lucía, are you sure you don't want anything to eat before you try to heal Vicente?" Mrs. Rodríguez asked as she gave Lucía the glass of water.

"Gracias, but not right now," Lucía answered. "I feel strong today."

Mrs. Rodríguez smiled and watched her drink the glass of water. She thought that Lucía looked much older than sixty, more like in her early eighties. She looked old and tired, but her eyes still had a sparkle.

"I think I'm ready to meet your son," Lucía said. "I'd like to see if I can heal your boy with God's help."

The women got up and Mrs. Rodríguez led the way to Vicente's room. Lucía carried her black suitcase and kept looking around as she walked through the house.

Vicente could hear light footsteps coming down the short hall. He tried to figure out who the third woman could be.

Mrs. Rodríguez gently knocked on the door. "Vicente, are you awake?" she asked, opening the door. Vicente couldn't believe his mother was bringing in his tía and the other woman without giving him a chance to brush his teeth or comb his hair. At least he was wearing pajamas. He sat up and scooted to the head of the bed, trying to make himself somewhat more presentable.

Viola went up to him and gave him a hug and a kiss.

"I am so sorry you're sick, mijito, but after today you're going to feel much better," Viola said with a smile.

Vicente smiled, not sure what his tía was talking about.

"Vicente, I want you to meet Lucía," his mother said. "She's from the Valley and she's here to cure you." Vicente nodded slowly. "From the Valley?"

"Sí, mijito, she came with me," Viola answered. "Lucía is Ana's mother, and Ana asked her to come here to cure you. Lucía is the best curandera in the Valley."

Vicente said nothing for a moment. He was trying to figure out what his mother was up to. Lucía stepped forward, closer to him, so he could get a better look at her. She smiled at him, and he felt as if he knew her.

"How do you feel, Vicente?" Lucía asked.

"Not too good," he said. "I am weak and I was coughing all night."

"Yes, he was coughing all night," Mrs. Rodríguez said.

Lucía walked up to him and put her hand on his forehead. "You feel hot," Lucía said. "Does your head hurt, too?"

"Yeah, a little bit," he replied.

Lucía stepped away and then turned to the women. "Becky, I need to talk to your son alone for a little while," she said. "I need to ask him some questions before I begin."

The women agreed to her request, but before leaving the room, Mrs. Rodríguez turned to Vicente and told him to do as Lucía asked. Lucía closed the door behind the women and picked up her black suitcase. She pulled a chair from behind Vicente's desk and sat down, putting the small case by her side.

Lucía said nothing for a moment and simply looked at Vicente. Such a handsome boy, she thought.

"How old are you, Vicente?" she asked.

"I'm twenty-one."

"Ah, Ana is just two years older than you," she said.

"Yeah, Ana is real nice," he said.

"Bueno, you are not doing so good, eh?" she said. "Your tía says that you are always getting sick. Is that true?"

Vicente readjusted himself in the bed. "Not always, but when I was kid I got real sick a couple of times."

Lucía nodded. "What kind of sick?"

"Well, I got pneumonia twice."

"Twice?" Lucía raised her brow.

"Yeah, they say if you get it once it's easy to get again," Vicente said.

"Ah, bueno. ¿Qué más?"

"So I got pneumonia twice, and I'm allergic to a lot of stuff, and I had my appendix taken out when I was about thirteen," Vicente said. "Then there was the time I almost had knee surgery, but I didn't."

"You have bad knees?" Lucía asked.

"No, I don't have bad knees. It's that I fell down and twisted my leg," he said. "It's OK now."

"How did you fall down?"

"I was being chased by a dog and it bit me and I fell," he said.

"The dog bit you on the same leg?" she asked.

Vicente sighed. "No, he bit my butt."

"Ah, that hurts," she said.

Vicente nodded. Lucía sat and wondered how such a young man could have such bad health and bad luck.

"Did you ever break a bone, like your arm or something?" she asked.

"Yeah, I have had a couple of fingers broken, my right arm, and my left foot," he said.

Lucía nodded her head as if to say, "Go on."

Vicente wondered how much more medical history this woman would want. He sighed again. He held out his right arm and with his left hand held the last two fingers on his right hand.

"I broke these two fingers playing baseball when I was in Little League," he said. "I was up to bat and the pitcher pitched the ball and it hit my two fingers."

Lucía made a face of disbelief. "And your arm?" Vicente nodded. "Yes. I broke my arm jumping hurdles when I was in track in high school."

Lucía frowned and shook her head. "You fell down?" she asked.

"Yeah, I fell down. I was running, and when I jumped I didn't jump high enough, and my legs got caught in the hurdle somehow, and me and the hurdle got all twisted up, and somehow my arm got caught in the hurdle and it broke," Vicente said, moving his hands around trying to explain how the accident occurred.

Again Lucía shook her head slowly. Why did this boy have such bad luck, she thought to herself. Vicente looked at her and began to wonder how he had managed to stay alive this long.

"¿Y tu foot?" she asked.

Vicente sighed. "Yeah, my foot. Well, when I was ten years old, my father died and . . ."

Lucía's body stiffened. "I thought your father was still alive."

"No, my ex-stepfather is still alive, but my real father is dead."

Lucía looked at the floor and thought for a moment.

"What was his name?"

"My real rather or my stepfather?" Vicente asked.

"Your real father," she said.

"Román Guzmán, and my stepfather is Luis Rodrí—" Román Guzmán. The name sent Lucía back twenty-two years to the time of her dark, evil soul. Her body chilled as she felt her weak heart let out a sad cry. She closed her eyes and thought, How many more, God? How many more wrongs must she endure for her foolish past? Maybe it wasn't the same man. Maybe this boy's curse would not strike her. She opened her eyes and saw the confusion in the boy's face. She regained her composure.

"Perdóname, please tell me what you were saying."

"Are you all right? Do you want some water or something?" Vicente asked.

"No, I'm OK. Just tell me what you were saying."

Vicente shrugged his shoulders and went on. "Well, when my father died, I wanted to be one of the pallbearers. My mother didn't want me to because she thought I couldn't lift the casket, but I did OK. But my tío, who was right behind me, well, he was drunk and lost his balance and fell and then everybody lost their balance and fell, and we dropped the casket. I tried to hang on, and the casket fell on my left foot and broke it."

Lucía put her hands on her face and slowly brought them down around her mouth. Vicente could see the woman's eyes watering. Her eyes closed, and a tear followed the lines down her cheek. She mumbled something in Spanish and thought of the hate that once filled her soul. So much hate she had had for him that she had cursed the innocent. What kind of woman would do that to the innocent? "Perdóname, Dios. Por favor, perdóname," she said into her warm hands.

She opened her eyes and wiped her tears. Vicente couldn't figure out what was wrong with this woman. Again she regained her composure.

"Vicente, do you have a picture of your real father?" Vicente was getting confused and his head was throbbing. "Yes, do you want to see it?"

Lucía nodded. Vicente got up, walked to his closet, and took down a photo album. He sat down and thumbed through the pages. He took out a picture and handed it to Lucía. "That's my father."

Lucía looked at the old photograph. He looked just as she remembered him. That coyote smile and the thick, dark hair. What woman wouldn't love him and then hate him? She looked at his son. He would be proud of such a fine young man.

She could see that Ana had her father's eyes. How could she have cursed Ana's father? How could she have cursed his son? She could feel her body trembling.

"Vicente, are you having bad dreams?" she asked.

"What?"

"In your dreams, is a woman trying to get you?"

"Yes," he said.

Lucía picked up her black suitcase, opened it, and took out a small change purse. She opened it and took out a photograph of herself when she was much younger. It was an old picture with bent corners and cracks running across it. She gave it to Vicente. "Do you know this woman?"

Vicente knew her. "This is her! This is the woman who is chasing me. How did you know?" he asked in disbelief.

Lucía took a deep breath and got up. "I can cure you. I need to talk to your mother. You lie back down. I can cure you, but first I need to talk to your mother."

Vicente began to speak, but Lucía looked at him and in a firm voice told him to lie down. This time Vicente said nothing.

Lucía left the room and walked into the living room, where Mrs. Rodríguez and Viola were sitting. As she entered, they stood up. "Is he OK, Lucía? I pray that you can help him," Mrs. Rodríguez said.

Lucía sat down and the two women sat down as well. Lucía said nothing for a few seconds. She was trying to figure out how to explain it all.

"Your son has a very powerful curse on him. It is powerful because the curse on him was done in hate," Lucía said. "I can take the curse away, but both of you must promise me one thing. If you don't do as you promise, Ana might die."

Viola was stunned. "Ana? Why would Ana die?" she asked.

Lucía put her hands to her face and looked at the floor. She took a deep breath.

"Ana is not my daughter. She belonged to my sister, who died when Ana was born. Román Guzmán is Ana's father. When Román found out he got my sister pregnant, he stopped coming by and didn't even come to my sister's funeral. I was so mad and filled with hate for him that I put a powerful curse on him and his first son. That both of them have bad luck and bad health.

My curse killed Román and now it's killing your son." Lucía began to cry.

Mrs. Rodríguez and Viola were without words.

"I will take the curse off your son, but you both must promise me that after I take the curse off, you will do what I ask," Lucía said. "I don't want my Ana to suffer for my sins."

Mrs. Rodríguez and Viola nodded their heads slowly with a look of disbelief.

"What I am saying is true and God knows," Lucía said. She got up and went into Vicente's room. When she entered the room, he tried to get up.

"Be still, mijito, I am going to cure you of an evil curse," she said. "I will make your bad dreams go away."

Vicente said nothing and didn't move. He could feel the good in her. He wasn't afraid.

"Close your eyes and be still," she said. Lucía lit a white candle and then burned some incense. She began her prayer in Spanish. "Lo que yo deseo para ti, sobre mí ha de caer. Y la maldición se me ha de devolver." The room filled with the aroma of the burning plants. Vicente took a deep breath and could feel his body warm and his lungs fill with air. He felt lighter. Never had he felt so relaxed. She watched his chest rise and fall slowly. The smooth rhythm of his breathing told her that he was fast asleep.

In his dream Vicente could see her standing in an open field. He wasn't afraid anymore. She smiled at him and then she began to float in the air. Higher and higher she went, waving at him until her body disappeared in the clouds.

He looked to his side, and there was his father smiling. His father reached out and held Vicente's hand and they began walking.

Lucía saw the smile on Vicente's face and knew she was ready.

Mrs. Rodríguez and Viola were relieved to see Lucía come out of the room.

"He will be fine, gracias a Dios, but now we must go to church and pray," Lucía said. "Please, we must go now!"

"What about Vicente?" Mrs. Rodríguez asked.

"Don't wake him; he will be dreaming all night," Lucía said.

The women drove to Mrs. Rodríguez's church, St. Mary's. The late-afternoon sun illuminated the front of the church and its stained-glass windows, and the image of Christ rising poured across the pews. On entering the church, each of the women made the sign of the cross, and then Lucía told them what she needed.

"Now that I have taken the curse off your son, we must pray that it does not fall on Ana," Lucía said. "We must pray with all our strength that the curse comes back to me."

"What?" Mrs. Rodríguez said.

"Becky, Lucía is the one that put the curse on Vicente and Román," Viola said. "If she takes the curse off, it will come back to her or the person she loves the most."

"The curse might go to Ana, so we must pray that it comes back to me," Lucía said.

Mrs. Rodríguez looked at Lucía. "But if the curse falls on you, can you cure yourself?"

"Lucía has to take in the curse. If this curse is too powerful—" Viola tried to finish but was cut off.

"Ya, we don't have too much time," Lucía said. "We must pray that the curse comes back to me, por favor."

The women knelt in the first pew before the altar. Lucía looked at Mrs. Rodríguez and gave her a hug. "Gracias for letting me cure your son," she said. "I hope you can forgive me for what I did to your husband."

Lucía closed her eyes and began to pray. She asked for forgiveness and prayed for the soul of Román Guzmán and of her sister. She prayed for an end to all her past curses. She prayed that this was the last curse.

Her body became light and she began to fly. She saw herself praying and saw the smile on her face as her body fell back into the pew. Mrs. Rodríguez and Viola began shaking her gently, but Lucía kept on flying.

Heart-Shaped Cookies

I was raised in a small south Texas town, a one-Catholic-church town, Edcouch, Texas. As you entered Edcouch on Highway 107, the sign read ENTERING EDCOUCH, POPULATION 2,683. One mile later it read LEAVING EDCOUCH, POPULATION 2,683. But I don't think Edcouch really had that many people unless the sign took into account various farm animals and wandering pets.

I was no different from anyone else in Edcouch; I was Mexican American, spoke Spanish, and was Catholic. The Catholic church in Edcouch was St. Theresa, and it was in this church that I served as an altar boy.

The priest, Father Ortiz, loved me. I was his favorite altar boy, even though he once caught me and José Sosa eating a bag of unblessed Eucharist wafers. (Holy cookies, Joe and I liked to call them.)

I liked being an altar boy for two reasons. One, we were allowed to get out of school whenever Father Ortiz had to perform services at a funeral, which always meant a free lunch at the Dairy Queen. Two, every Sunday I had the chance to see just about everyone in Edcouch. Everyone except the "heathens," whom I saw at the five o'clock mass. The ten-o'clock mass, though, had the most people, including a couple of the high school cheerleaders, who had to stick out their soft pink tongues to receive the holy cookie. There I would stand next to Father Ortiz, with a small, round brass tray. When the girls would come up to accept the sacrament, they would close their eyes and stick out their pink tongues. What a sight that was!

St. Theresa had some interesting parishioners. There was the mayor, the fat mailman, who didn't deliver letters (we only had post office boxes in Edcouch), the policeman and his alcoholic brother, a few volunteer firemen, Mr. and Mrs. Carson (who were really Methodists), and Mr. Garza, the owner of the panadería. I liked most of the people who went to church, except Mr. Garza. Not even Luis Luna, the school bully, who lived in the worst part of Edcouch, el rincón del diablo, was as mean as Mr. Garza.

During the collection part of the mass each altar boy would take one side of the pews. We only had two rows of pews, so we could cover the whole church. I always walked down the middle of the church and took the right side and always, always had to put the collection basket before Mr. Garza, who never gave a cent. The poorest woman in town, Miss Alvarado, who always wore a worn-out red shawl and an old pair of leather sandals and who only had three front teeth, always gave something. Even Luis Luna gave something, though it was probably stolen lunch money, but hey, he gave!

Anyway, Mr. Garza never gave. When I would put the collection basket in front of him, I would sometimes shake it a bit, but he wouldn't even flinch. This would go on and on Sunday after Sunday. I would tell all my friends what a "pinche vato" Mr. Garza was.

My mother, as well as everyone else in town, loved Mr. Garza's panadería, and she would send me down to Mr. Garza's every other day to buy molletes, empanadas, and marranitos. I had to admit that Mr. Garza had great pan dulce: heart-shaped cookies covered with sugar and cookies shaped like pigs were my favorites. As I pulled open the screen door to the bakery, a little bell above the door would jingle. You had to make sure the door closed behind you because Mr. Garza did not like flies in his bakery, and I don't think he liked me in his bakery, either. Mr. Garza knew who I was; he knew my parents and he always talked to my grandparents, but he never had anything to say to me. There he would stand behind the glass counter with his fat, hairy arms resting on it. On his fat wrist he wore a gold watch, and gold rings circled his short, fat fingers. His hair was always slicked back and was as black as the thin, wormy-looking mustache underneath his pug nose. He would look down at me and ask in a low voice, "¿Qué quieres esta mañana?" I would look in the glass cabinet filled with brightly colored molletes: pink, yellow, brown, red, and white. There were nice big brown marranitos, heart-shaped cookies covered with sugar, and pan dulce of all colors and shapes. I could feel my eyes dilating and my mouth watering. I would tell him what I wanted, pay him, and leave without saying any more than I had to. But I would make sure I was halfway home before I began eating the cookies because I did not want Mr. Garza to see me.

What probably made me the angriest was watching him drive by in his yellow Chevrolet Impala with his windows rolled up on the hottest days. Mr. Garza had a car with an eight-track tape player, a defroster, a heater, and an air conditioner, and they all worked.

One cold day after Mass, Father Ortiz invited the altar boys to his house right next to the church for hot Mexican chocolate and pan dulce. It was an invitation we couldn't refuse, and besides, you can't say no to a priest.

We were having a great time until I asked—knowing the answer—where he bought the cookies.

"What? I can't believe you bought the cookies from Mr. Garza's panadería," I immediately said. Father looked a little puzzled.

"Why, David, you don't like Mr. Garza's cookies?" he asked in his priestlike voice.

"No, I like the cookies. It's Mr. Garza I don't like, and you shouldn't like him, either."

"Why don't you like Mr. Garza, David? Has he done something to hurt you?"

"No, it's just that he never gives money to the church. Whenever I put the basket in front of him, he just sits there."

Father looked a little upset and I knew why. I knew better: God doesn't care if you give money to the church or not, even if you are as rich as Mr. Garza. But instead of giving me the standard lecture, Father Ortiz asked to follow him to his office. I figured he was going to give me the lecture in his office instead of in front of the other altar boys.

Once we were inside his office, Father Ortiz brought out a big black book, one I had never seen before. It was full of names and I recognized all of them. They were parishioners of St. Theresa. Some of the names were in blue ink and others in red ink. Father pointed to Mr. Garza's name, which was in blue ink, and on the same line, a couple of inches across, was written the amount of $20,800.

"David, that's how much Mr. Garza has given to St. Theresa over the past eight years," Father said. "Do you know why he has given so much to the church?"

All I could do was shake my head—no.

"Nine years ago Mr. Garza's wife, Elena, became very ill and was dying. Mr. Garza and I prayed together all night for Elena. Mr. Garza made a promesa. Mr. Garza promised he would give the church fifty dollars a week for the rest of his life if God would let Elena live another year. Elena died four months after Mr. Garza made the promise."

I couldn't say anything. I felt terrible and asked Father to forgive me, but he said Mr. Garza was the one from whom I should ask forgiveness. After I found out about Mr. Garza's donations, I stopped shaking the collection basket in front of him, and I wouldn't say mean things about him to anyone. But I still could not say I was sorry for the things I thought. Weeks passed and months went and then years, but I could not bring myself to apologize.

Oh, I tried a couple of times, but I just couldn't. Mr. Garza died three years ago, and marranitos and heart-shaped sugar cookies have never tasted the same since.

FLASH
FICTION

The Death of a Writer

In fourth grade our English teacher, Ms. Ayala, wanted us to write a short story. She said the best story would win a bag of pan dulce. When she said that, every kid in the class smiled with wide eyes. It had to be a story like Robinson Crusoe. We had to pretend we were shipwrecked on a deserted island, and then describe what we would do.

It was hard for us to imagine, because none of us had ever been on a ship and the only island we had been on was Padre Island. But Ms. Ayala said, "That's what imagination is for. You can write anything you want."

"Anything?" we asked.

"Yes, anything," she said with a warm, trusting smile.

I thought about it all morning and during lunch. On the playground, my friends and I were playing marbles, and all I could talk about was the story we had to write. Ramiro Ramos, who was burning ants with matches he had snuck into school, looked up from his favorite hobby.

"You heard her. She said we could write about anything we want. We can't get in trouble for writing what we want to write," he said as ants curled to a hot flame.

A few days later our teacher started inviting students to read their stories out loud in front of the class. I can't remember any of them, not even my own story, but I do remember Ramiro's.

When she called him, he got up and walked in front the class and took out a folded sheet of paper from his back pocket. He unfolded it several times and cleared his throat.

"This is my story," he said. "One day I was on a ship and it crashed on an island. There was this monster and it ate me. The end."

I started laughing because I thought it was the funniest story ever, but the other students looked confused. Ms. Ayala got mad and sent Ramiro to the principal's office, and he was paddled three times.

Scary Heroes

I was a confident seven-year-old, walking with my older cousins. We were lost together, looking for my mother and Tía. The annual livestock show always stunk of cow caca and hay. It was held on acres of fields outside of Mercedes, Texas, about ten miles from Edcouch, my hometown. Half the livestock show was just that, livestock: cows, pigs, and piles of caca. The other half was covered with carnival rides, spinning and flipping with happy screams.

There were people everywhere, and we decided to split up and meet at the House of Horrors. My cousin and I walked for less than a moment and then I lost him in the crowd, but I wasn't worried because I found myself in front of a carnival game. People with big zipper ride smiles tossing nickels onto colorful plates. The coins would make beautiful champagne-glass-clicking-sounds and skip off the shiny plates.

Then there was the cotton candy machine, whipping pink string around paper sticks. The sweet aroma pushed away the dry livestock stench, and my mouth began to water, but I had no money. That's when I remembered that I was lost. I walked to the House of Horrors and looked around, but I didn't see my family anywhere. I waited for what seemed an hour and began to worry. The spooky laughs from the House of Horrors gave me a cold chill and I decided to walk to our family car and wait for my mother. My father was in the National Guard and he was assigned to parking cars. I thought maybe I'd see him directing traffic.

The parking lot was a dark dirt field covered in cars. The farther I walked away from the carnival rides the more the screams sounded terrified. I found our car and sat on the roof, letting my legs rest on the windshield. I hummed a little bit, trying to drown out the swirled screams and twisted carnival music, but it was no use. I began to sniffle and then tears rolled down my face. I was lost, and no one was looking for me.

I walked back to the carnival crying. Now everything was a blur and then I heard glass shattering into laughter. I saw two boys throwing beer bottles at a telephone pole. I stopped and stood, still crying, with my head being raised by my heavy sighs.

They stopped laughing and walked up to me. I noticed they were smoking. One of them took a slow drag and let the smoke pour out of his mouth. The smoke surrounded his face and he leaned out of the cloud over me and asked me in a gruff voice, "Hey, little boy. Are you lost?"

I looked up at the dark figure and nodded, "I can't find my mother," I said.

They looked at each other, but I couldn't see their faces. One of them took a final drag of his cigarette, making the end of it a fire-red that reflected in his eyes. Then he flicked it into the darkness. He put his hand out, and though I was afraid, I reached out. The other boy took my other hand, and we walked into the bright carnival lights. They walked me to the lost and found booth, and they told the lady they found me walking around the parking lot. The lady smiled, and then a policeman walked up, and the two boys bolted like rabbits. The policeman shouted and chased them. Then my mother and father appeared. They were arguing over who should have been watching over me. That's when I realized I had angels watching me.

It's What You Sew

My father didn't like it when my grandmother, Mamá Locha, taught me how to sew. Because before long, I was laying down patterns and learning how to make dresses. Often I was a human doll for dresses Mamá Locha was making. I'd stand still as she made final measurements with safety pins. It drove my father nuts.

One afternoon as I modeled a dress for Mamá Locha, Dad walked in with a long narrow box wrapped in brown butcher paper and handed it to me.

"What is it?" I asked.

"Something every eight-year-old boy should have. Open it," he said proudly.

I took quickly took off the wrapper and there it was, a brand new Daisy BB rifle. My grandmother gasped. "Esa cosa es peligrosa," she said.

My father nodded. "Yes, but you know what's more dangerous? A boy walking around in a girl's dress."

My BB gun needed no reloading for fifty shots and every telephone pole, tree, can, bottle, street sign, streetlight, bird, dog, and cat knew it.

I was a fast shooter and couldn't carry enough BBs. That's when my sewing talent came to the rescue. I called my grandmother and asked her if the sewing machine was available, she said yes. Dad overheard my brief conversation.

"Where are you going?"

"I'm going to Mamá Locha's house," I said.

I grabbed my BB gun and a big box of BBs and bounced out the door. I showed my grandmother a sketch of what I wanted to make, and she frowned but didn't say no.

"As long as you're sewing," she said.

I walked into her sewing room and went through her box of scraps, and began sewing. I was halfway done when my dad came in the room.

He leaned over and our eyes met for a moment through the stabbing needle of the Singer, "Mijo, why are you sewing?" he asked.

Without looking up, I answered him, "Well, Dad, you know how Davy Crockett carried that pouch filled with gunpowder across his chest?"

Dad nodded, "Yeah."

"Well, I'm going to make a pouch for my BBs. This way I can carry twice as many."

Dad smiled, stood up and patted my shoulder. "That's my boy," he said.

Dad Shoots to Kill

When Hurricane Beulah hit the Rio Grande Valley in September of 1967, my dad was ready. It didn't matter if Beulah had sustained winds of 140 miles per hour, and that tens of thousands of people had evacuated the Texas Gulf coast, my dad had his orders. Dad was in the National Guard and had orders to pick up his machine gun, leave his family, and head down to Brownsville to protect the stores from possible looters.

Dad was in his army fatigues packing his green duffel bag as I talked.

"So, you just walk around the streets?" I asked.

"Those are my orders. To patrol the streets and secure calm and order," Dad said with firm purpose.

"But Mom said no one is there because of the hurricane," I said.

"No, mijito, there may be people trying to break into the stores and steal things."

"So, if someone is robbing a store and they shoot at you, are you going to shoot them back?"

My dad stood upright, "Hell, yeah, if someone tries to kill me, you bet I'll try to kill them."

That night Hurricane Beulah made landfall, dropping walls of rain. Mom opened the front door so we could see the lake around us. Our covered front cement porch was under water, and though our house was on cinder blocks, the floodwaters were just inches under our house. The water around us moved like the ocean. I thought maybe we were in a boat and that we'd float away.

My mother held my two-year-old brother in one arm and put her other arm around my shoulders. She looked very worried. "We may have to leave this house tonight," she said.

All I could think of was my father killing someone.

Man vs. Beast

Up to the age of ten, I wasn't afraid of jellyfish. How could I be afraid of a floating balloon? They don't have teeth or claws. Sure, they have tentacles, but not like an octopus. When I was a kid I saw drawings of an octopus taking down a whole ship. So what could a floating marshmallow do to me?

I was at Padre Island with my family and cousins. My brother and I and older girl cousins, Ana and Millie, were knee-deep in the water on a sandbar. We saw the translucent purple jellyfish floating by. It looked just like the illustrations I had seen in schoolbooks.

"Let's pop it," my brother said in evil excitement.

"Yeah," I said. "Too bad we don't have our BB guns. We could pop it from here."

Our cousins frowned and Ana spoke up. "Look, that jellyfish is not bothering anyone. It's harmless, so leave it alone," she said as if she was our mother.

My brother was quick. "It's not harmless. It's got tentacles and they sting you all over."

"Yeah," I said. "And it's heading straight for the shore where little kids are playing!" I said in a fake panicked tone.

My brother followed my suit. "We've got to save them," he said as Superman would, and we ran and dived off the sandbar. We heard our cousin shout, "You guys are idiots!" but we kept splashing and swimming.

Once we got to the shore we ran to our dad's truck and grabbed a shovel and a hoe we had brought to make sand castles, but popping jellyfish sounded like more fun. We ran to our father and mother, who were sitting with our tío and tía in lawn chairs. Dad and Tío were both wearing cheap sunglasses, smoking cigarettes, and drinking beer.

"Hey, Dad, we're going to pop a jellyfish!" my brother said.

Our mother looked up from her magazine. "Those things can sting you. Just leave it alone."

Our tío started laughing. "'Tan locos! You got to have real guts to go after a jellyfish," he said. "I dare you to do it." My dad started laughing too, but our mother didn't think it was funny.

"Honey, tell them to leave the jellyfish alone," she said as she pushed on his shoulder.

"But Mom, it's attacking the shore," my brother said. "We've got to stop it."

Mom nudged Dad again. "Tell them no."

"But Tío just dared us. We have to do it," I said.

Then her brother, our tío, jumped in again. "They must learn. Man versus beast. Let them go."

"It's not a beast; it's just a jellyfish," my brother said. "It doesn't have teeth or nothing."

"Y los tentacles?" our tío asked. We shrugged.

"OK, OK. Two boys against one jellyfish," Dad said. "Good luck, boys." And he waved us off.

We ran into the warm gulf water, I with the shovel, and my brother with the hoe. We were chest-deep when we encountered the sea creature bobbing up and down and swaying from side to side. We surrounded the jellyfish, counted to three, and brought down our weapons upon the floating bag of air. We thought maybe we'd hear the jellyfish pop, but all we heard was metal clacking sounds of the shovel and hoe. I scooped up the deflated purple body and brought it to shore.

My dad and tío met us, and Dad said to put the jellyfish in the trashcan. And as we did we noticed how long its tentacles were—too long. Then I saw my brother's back covered in red lines and when he turned around he saw that my chest and stomach were covered with red lines too. Our skinny legs were striped in red ribbons and then we felt the burning between our legs. We ran to our mother, but she just put her hand up and said, "¿Quién te manda? Go see your father."

Our Dad and tío were done with their first six-pack. We showed them our red bodies and told them how it was burning between our legs but they just laughed at us. Dad gave us a bottle of lotion and told us to rub it everywhere we itched. We lay spread-eagle on a beach towel baking in the hot sun. Our tipsy tío walked over to us and put out his arms as if he were a balancing scale.

"Let's see, man versus beast, beast always wins and you learned the hard way. You don't need teeth to bite," he said and started clapping and laughing.

Me, the Good Kid

In fourth grade I started a fight between Flaco Flores and Nacho Negrete, two kids who were always fighting each other. It was during Mrs. De la Garza's class. She was my mother's bowling partner and I saw her every Wednesday night at the bowling alley, so I had to be extra nice in her class.

One afternoon the whole class was quiet, doing their assigned work. I sat in the row against the wall and finished my work pretty fast and was waiting for everyone else. I got bored and noticed that Flaco and Nacho were actually doing their work. They sat in the row next to mine: Flaco in the front seat, Sulema behind him (she sat across from me, but she was absent that day), and then Nacho.

Flaco had his face down and I could see his pencil scribbling away and every now and then he'd scratch his head like he was thinking or feeling for lice. Nacho had his face down too, all scrunched up with his tongue sticking out and his fingers deep red from pressing the pencil down too hard.

I took two pieces of paper and made two tight paper balls. I threw one at Flaco, hitting him on the back of his head, and quickly threw one at Nacho, hitting him in the face. Flaco spun around and Nacho looked, slamming his pencil down.

Flaco shot up and they exchanged several bad words in Spanish and then Flaco grabbed Nacho's desk and flipped it over. Nacho wrestled himself out of his desk and sprang up like a cat on Flaco. Mrs. De la Garza shouted for them to stop, and then yelled at the top of her lungs for Coach Villalobos.

The door flew open and Coach Villalobos, a soldier who had fought in the war and was as big as a gorilla, charged in like a hurricane, grabbed Flaco and Nacho by their collars, shook them like rag dolls, and dragged them out of the classroom to the principal's office, where they were paddled.

Mrs. De la Garza regained her composure and adjusted her hair and told us to complete our assignment. After twenty minutes, Flaco and Nacho came in and took their seats gingerly. I thought it was pretty funny, but I also felt pretty guilty. I walked up to Mrs. De la Garza's desk.

"Mrs. De la Garza, I have a confession to make," I said.

She smiled pleasantly at me. "Yes?"

"Well," I sighed. "You know that fight Flaco and Nacho got into?"

"Of course, I was right here when it happened."

"Well, I started it."

She smiled kindly, "I know they're your friends and you're trying to help them. Now go sit down."

"But Miss, it's my fault. See, I took two paper wads and threw one at the back of Flaco's head and then I threw one at Nacho and they thought they did it, so they got into a mistake fight."

She smiled, "I believe you. But those two need to be paddled every day."

Humming Forever

Could I shoot a hummingbird? I had shot everything else in sight: doves, crows, sparrows, dogs, cats, ants, locusts, and even dragonflies. But a hummingbird is no more than two inches long and flies in quick zigzag jolts. And they're hard to find too.

I knew of a bright blue hummingbird two blocks from my house. One Friday, walking home after school, I decided to take a different road and saw Mrs. Flores staring at something in her flower bush. She was the oldest woman in town and lived by herself, and always gave out the best Halloween candy. Her lawn was covered with every plant that had flowers. When you walked by her house, it was like walking by the women's perfume department in a big store, but the scents didn't sting your nose; they made you dizzy.

I stopped to watch her and she caught my eye and waved me over, but gestured for me to be quiet. I wasn't sure what she was looking at and as I walked up to her very slowly, she pointed at the bush. I followed the imaginary line from her crooked bony finger to a hovering hummingbird.

We watched it dart from flower to flower, and then dash away with a blur. Mrs. Flores smiled, "Isn't that bird beautiful?"

I nodded. "Yes, Mrs. Flores. Does it live in this bush?"

"I'm not sure where he lives, but I always see him in the morning when I'm watering the flowers. I think he likes flowers with dew flavor." She smiled and brought her hands together in thanks.

I went home and practiced shooting wooden clothespins off the clothesline. They were about the size of a hummingbird, but they were still. Hummingbirds never are. When I'd shoot I noticed the BB coming out of the barrel would have a slight curve and I kept missing the clothespin. This called for my pellet rifle. The soft lead pellets were more expensive but I needed complete accuracy.

I went inside the house and Mom was cooking in the kitchen.

"What are you doing?" she asked in a suspicious tone.

"Nothing, I'm just going to shoot some cans with my pellet gun."

She narrowed her eyes and nodded, "Huerco, you better be shooting cans."

My pellet rifle was a straight shooter and I broke every clothespin on the clothesline. My mother came outside, saw what I had done, and shook her head. She called me huerco zonzo.

I borrowed my father's travel alarm clock and set it for sunrise. When I left the house everyone was still asleep and outside it was cool and peaceful, and there was still dew on the plants. A good sign, I thought.

I strolled the quiet streets with my pellet gun and hoped that Mrs. Flores was not watering her plants. I walked by her house slowly and when I didn't see her, I walked into her yard and went straight to the bush.

I kept one eye on the front of her house and one eye on the bush, searching for the blue bird. I stood very still and then I saw it float and weave between the thin twigs. I took aim at the chest, followed the fast wings for a minute, and then fired. The wings stopped and the humming bird fell like a feather.

I picked up the little body and felt the warmth in my palm, and then, an overwhelming sense of guilt. I needed someone to yell at me. I needed someone to tell me what I did was wrong. I sat on Mrs. Flores's concrete porch, so when she stepped out and saw that I had killed her flower bird she could wring my neck.

Dove Lesson

When I was twelve years old, I was awakened one morning by a dove outside my bedroom window. It just wouldn't stop singing, and I wanted to get back to sleep. After a few minutes, I got up, grabbed my faithful BB gun, walked to the back door, and took steady aim. I shot. Easy. The dove dropped like a rock.

Going back to my bedroom, I heard my grandfather call out to me. I opened his door but made sure he didn't see my BB gun. He lit his pipe and then asked me what I had done. I wanted to lie, but it was too difficult.

"Well, I . . . I was asleep and then this stupid bird started making all this racket. So I took my BB gun and shot it."

My grandfather was an emotional man. His eyes began to fill. "David, do you know what that dove was doing? It was singing a beautiful song that no other animal can sing. A song that me or you could never sing. A song that God taught it to sing. And you went and killed it."

I tried to say something, but couldn't find the words. He told me to close his door, and I did. I leaned against the wall and stared at my BB gun, then put it in my room and went outside.

I looked at the dove, then picked it up and held its still-warm body. I got a shovel and dug a small hole and placed the bird in it. I took two twigs from the tree the bird had been singing in and made a cross to put at the head of the grave. I cried for a bit and told God I was sorry, and promised that I would never again kill any living animal as long as I lived.

The incident didn't make me get rid of my BB gun, but all I shot from then on were bottles, cans, and, once, my foot.

Bombs Away

For show and tell, I took a bomb to school. My fourth-grade teacher said we could bring anything we wanted, and it was just lying around the garage for years doing nothing but rusting. My father had brought it home after a weekend of playing soldier. He was in the National Guard and always brought home cool things, like army food, army makeup, blank bullets, flares, and bombs.

It was a dummy shell, so it was harmless but heavy. I picked it up and dropped it in the backyard and grabbed the water hose. I took some soap and a steel-wool pad, and began brushing off the rust. My mother came outside and saw what I was doing. I told her what I was going to do with it and she raised her brow.

"You can't take a bomb. Want to blow up the whole town?"

Then Dad spoke up as he walked through the back screen door. "It's a dud, that thing can't blow up anything."

My mom shook her head. "'Tas bien loco."

Dad and I bought some red and silver spray paint and painted the bomb; a silver case with a bright red point. I carried it to school in a paper bag and in class I didn't let anyone see it. I watched students take up really dumb stuff like a lava lamp, a magic wand that didn't work, and a frog some kid had caught in his backyard. The kids in the class were mildly amused, but I knew my bomb would blow them away.

When the teacher called my name I walked up as if I was holding a baby. I put the bag down on the floor, and took out the bomb and all the kids started to get out of their seats to get a better look. Our teacher had lots of knickknacks on her desk like a wooden apple, paper clip containers, a little school bus, and her favorite, a snow globe of a tiny village surrounded with pine trees. She made some space on her desk and as I gently tried to put the bomb down, somehow I lost my footing and banged it against the desk. All her things fell off, and then I dropped the bomb on the desk. All the students gasped and a couple of girls even screamed.

I tried to calm the students and said, "Don't worry. It's safe; it's a dud. It can't do anything."

The bomb fell on its side and began to roll and I froze in fear. In slow motion the bomb rolled off the desk and landed point first on the peaceful snow globe village. OK, so I was wrong.

THE PLAY

Preface

In 2002 I was an actor in Austin, Texas, doing what I thought was powerful and meaningful work. I was also the artistic director of an upstart progressive theater company, Nushank Theater. Our goal was to hit the audience as powerfully as possible with realistic and thought-provoking material. I guess you could say my attitude was brash with a hint of nineteen twenties arrogance. Our shows were successful and we were developing a following. The company was being covered by the local media and I was feeling good about it and myself.

One day a writer friend of mine, David Rice, handed me a copy of *Crazy Loco,* which was a book of short stories. I liked the cover art, but it didn't move me enough to open the book. However, my friend continued to push me to read it and was so persistent that at one point I wanted to punch him in the nose. Then I thought about it and realized that my friend David Rice was a respected, published author, so I read it.

After a few days, Rice wanted to meet and discuss one of the stories in the book because he thought it would make a great play. I didn't like the idea and was nervous. I hadn't liked the story and furthermore, I didn't do "children's shows." Doing that sort of work seemed like something only part-time actors did when they couldn't find any other work.

I met with Rice anyway and he could tell that I wasn't 100 percent sold on the idea, but he was not deterred. He presented me with graphs and statistics that showed the high dropout rate of students in the Rio Grande Valley. Rice talked in circles and in rhyme and metaphor; he repeated and threatened. He spoke of previous Mexican American generations who had never had opportunities and tried to make me feel guilty. He badgered me until I finally agreed to reread his story.

So I did read his story again and I didn't feel any different. It was the kind of story I had heard a thousand times and seen happen to many of my friends. It was about a talented young girl from the Rio Grande Valley whose parents didn't want her to leave the nest for greater opportunities. It seemed to me that this story had already been told many times, so I blew it off. Furthermore, I felt that it was beneath my artistic sensibilities.

A week later I went home to McAllen, Texas, to visit my mother. I happened to have Rice's book with me, so I gave it to her and told her about Rice's idea. She liked the cover, so she went to the bedroom with the book. After a while she walked into the living room where I was channel surfing and I saw that she was crying. She said, "Mijito, this is my story. You have to write this play!" I was shocked that she loved the story so much, so I sat down at the kitchen table with her and discussed it. She told me her own story, which was remarkably similar: her parents hadn't let her go to college for exactly the same reasons as those of the parents in the story. This was something I had not known, and I began to realize that Rice was on to something and that the lead character in the play was exactly like my mother as a girl. So I went back to Austin and told Rice I would write the play.

I read the story yet again, broke it down, and wrote the play in two weeks. Rice secured funding with GEAR UP at UT Pan American University for a tour of the play in the Rio Grande Valley. The premiere was a success, and soon we got calls from organizations all over the country that wanted us to perform the play. We traveled to Washington, DC, Florida, New Mexico, and Colorado and performed the play for thousands of students and parents.

The story and play are both titled "She Flies." It is the story of Milagros and her journey from her humble home to college. Milagros's journey is as improbable as my writing and performing it, but both were accomplished. It's amusing to look back on my initial reluctance, but now I love this play and I love performing it, especially for audiences of students and parents. I always imagine that my mother is the main character and that her parents are in the audience.

Thank you, David Rice, for convincing me to do this. I would also like to thank my beloved wife, Erin, who gave me the idea for the Raúl character; to Raúl Castillo for allowing me to use his tagging monologue; to Gear Up UT Pan American, without whose support this play would not have been possible; and to God's army: you know who you are.

Mike D. García

CAST OF CHARACTERS

MILAGROS

MILAGROS'S MOTHER

MILAGROS'S FATHER, DAVID

BUS DRIVER

LEILA

RAÚL

ENGLISH TEACHER, MR. FLORES

TÍA MANA

COLLEGE RECRUITER, CHARLES MACINTYRE

She Flies

Adapted for the stage by Mike D. García © 2002
Based on David Rice's short story "She Flies"
from *Crazy Loco*, 2001.

1

Play begins with lights up center stage. We are in Milagros's home. Milagros begins scene with a sense of urgency; she is trying to get ready for school and is running out of time. Set pieces include kitchen table and chair.

MILAGROS: Mom.

There is no answer.

MILAGROS: Mom! . . . Mom! *(At this point Milagros is screaming.)* MOM!

MOM: *(Quietly.)* Yes?

MILAGROS: Where's my faded blue jeans? *(Rummaging through a laundry basket.)*

MOM: In the dryer.

MILAGROS: They weren't dirty.

MOM: They were on the floor.

MILAGROS: Ay, Mom!

MOM: Come eat your cereal. Your corn flakes are getting all soggy.

MILAGROS: Thanks, I'll be there in a second. . .

Mom goes over to the kitchen table humming and picks up the newspaper. Starts to read.

MOM: Nope . . . ugly . . . too short . . . too fat . . . too hairy . . . Y esta, qué perra . . .

MILAGROS: What are you talking about? *(Walks over to the table.)*

MOM: The pageant.

MILAGROS: Oh, the Miss Grapefruit or is it Miss Watermelon? I forget.

MOM: No, it's the Miss Citrus. You know, when I was young . . .

MILAGROS: I know, Mom. You've told me a million times. You were Miss Citrus Queen runner-up. Let it go. That was like a thousand years ago.

MOM: Milagros, I was pushed out. There is no justice in our society.

MILAGROS: Mom, it's too early for pageant talk, please.

MOM: Milagros, are your pants wet?

MILAGROS: *(Quickly gets up from the table.)* Gotta go . . .

MOM: Did you get those from the dryer?

MILAGROS: They're my favorite. They'll be dry by the time I get to school.

MOM: Ay, mija, no tienes vergüenza. Your pompis are going to freeze, then you're going to catch a cold and die of pneumonia.

MILAGROS: Bye, Mom. I love you, too.

MOM: Hurry up, Milagros, before you miss the bus!

Sound cue of bus horn and music for the next scene. Milagros walks off wet and waddling. Lights fade out. Quick change. Cast hit their marks quickly. Bus Driver music starts.

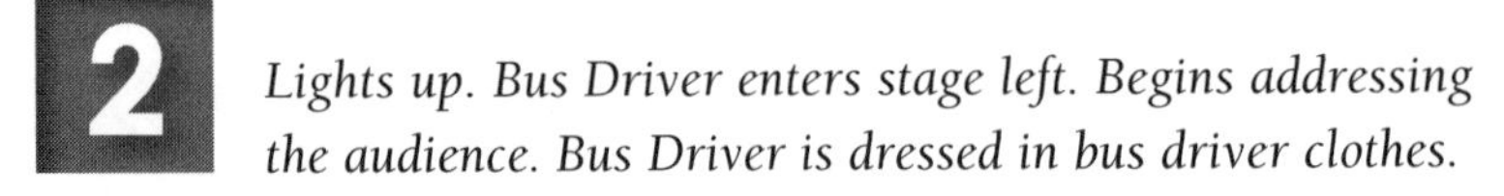

2

Lights up. Bus Driver enters stage left. Begins addressing the audience. Bus Driver is dressed in bus driver clothes.

BUS DRIVER: Get on the bus, ya'll. We're going to school! To school you about things you may not know, or things you might not care to know. About things, things of consequence and things consequently concretely creative. I'm talking about you. You samurai warrior, you braniac, you sporty. You I'm-too-shy-to-talk-to-you-don't-look-at-me. I'm talking about you. My people. We. Us. *(Cast enters on their cue.)* Nosotros. The home team. My peeps. My homegirls and boys. I'm talking about you. Respect. You. Respect education. Go where few Latinos have gone. To the inner parts of the brain. Use it. Think. Be creative. Don't let time slip away. Life *is* like a box of chocolates!! I'm talking about you. I'm talking about you. I'm talking about you! Get on the bus, ya'll. We're going to school . . . We're going to school.

Sound cue: music fades out. Cast makes their way off stage. Lights out. Bus Driver music fades. Pause. Monologue music begins.

3

Lights up. Milagros does entire scene down center. Prerecorded music plays throughout scene. Music note: sound cues: party voices, kids laughing, parakeets fluttering their wings. Mariachis in the background. Setting up party. As scene escalates so does the energy of the sound track. Milagros, with this monologue, needs to bring the audience into her world. Paint these images.

MILAGROS: One of my earliest memories is of setting free more than 300 parakeets. It was my fifth birthday, and my parents had thrown me a party at Tía Mana Garza's house. Tía Mana had made me a dress and bought me matching shoes and a hat. *(Sound cue: kids laughing, light mariachi music.)* She had decorated her backyard with ribbons tied to the trees and her two birdcages. One cage was filled with hundreds of parakeets. *(Sound cue: a few bird sounds.)* It was eight feet high and ten feet across, covered in chicken wire with holes so small that I could barely fit my little finger through them. The other cage held Tía's favorite possession: a green and red parrot named Pájaro. *(Sound cue: Pájaro saying, "Milagros, qué bonita.")* Pájaro wore an ankle band attached to kite string so he wouldn't escape. Whenever Tía let him out of his cage, he walked to the top and stretched his wings. Sometimes he'd flutter them and then fly straight up at full speed, but the string would snap him down.

During my birthday party I walked up to the big parakeet cage with a cookie. I thought maybe I'd push the cookie under the cage door and see if the parakeets would eat it. Tía

Mana had more colors in her big birdcage than there were in my biggest box of crayons. Some of the parakeets would fly back and forth really fast, *(sound cue: fluttering of wings)* hitting the cage with their bodies. Others would clutch the walls with their claws, and with their beaks they'd bite the cage wire. To me they looked as if they were trying to tear out of the cage. I think I felt sorry for them. Whenever I walked up to their cage, they turned their little heads and stared at me, fluttering their wings hard against the cage.

I turned around and looked at Tía Mana, who was watering her azaleas. She smiled at me but said nothing. I tried to push the cookie through the slit under the cage door, but it was too narrow. As I lifted the latch of the door, I heard my parents in the distance, telling me to stop. But I didn't want to stop.

I pulled the door open, and the sound of hundreds of singing birds swept away the shouts of my parents. *(Voice-over from offstage: "Milagros, no!")* The parakeets flew out, and I felt as if I were floating *(sound cue: wisp of wind)* in a rainbow. They swirled around me, their feathers grazing my face, chest, shoulders, and arms. I wanted to float away with them. I could hear them whispering to me as they darted by. I lifted my arms and stood on the tips of my toes, wondering if I was about to fly. The birds swooped into the trees of Tía's backyard, singing happily. Pájaro, on his kite string, sang too. And Tía Mana dropped the water hose and put her arms up, as if she were trying to embrace the flying colors. She was laughing, and her laugh was the same pitch as that of the singing birds. *(Sound cue: fainting bird sounds.)*

My father ran to me and slammed the cage door, *(sound cue: cage door closing)* but only a few birds still remained. He started yelling at me, but I couldn't understand him. He jabbed his finger inches from my face. I didn't know what he was so mad about. To me the parakeets wanted to be free, and Tía looked very happy watching them spread their tiny wings. I remember Dad saying, *(Voice-over: "Milagros, what are you thinking? The birds are escaping!")* Escaping. It was the only word I heard, over and over.

Soundtrack fades.

Then I felt Tía Mana's hands on my stomach. I looked up and she was standing behind me. She pulled me to her, and I could feel her warmth on my back.

"Milagros has done the right thing," she said. "I've had those birds too long. They should be free."

Lights go to black. Sound cue: hallway noise. School background noise. Monologue music fades into sounds of hallway.

4

Lights up on Milagros, Leila, and Raúl. They are seated at their desks. Raúl has his head down trying get a few last moments of sleep before class begins. The girls are removing their books from their bags, getting ready for class. Leila is looking at her compact mirror making sure she's looking satisfactory. Set: 3-4 desks.

MILAGROS: You look fine, Leila.

LEILA: You can't be too sure. What if Enrique Iglesias walked in?

MILAGROS: Or Brad Pitt.

LEILA: Ooh, he's gross! Besides, he probably doesn't like Valley girls.

MILAGROS: Neither does Enrique.

RAÚL: Would you all please shut up!! No one likes the both of you! I'm trying to sleep.

LEILA: *(Taunting Raúl.)* What? Are you afraid of, girls? *(Winking at him.)*

RAÚL: I'm not afraid of girls; I'm afraid of brujas! I've seen you fly around town on a broomstick.

MILAGROS: Watch out, she'll put a spell on you.

Raúl looks at the girls, smirks, then puts his head back down.

Leila mimes to Milagros that Raúl is loco. They laugh.

LEILA: Did you study for the quiz? Wait, of course you did, you always study.

MILAGROS: I was bored last night so I read. What, you didn't?

RAÚL: Brujas can't read.

LEILA: Shut up, Raúl!

Sound cue: Bell rings.

PRINCIPAL: *(Voice-over done live.)* Good morning, Raiders. This is your principal speaking. It's another warm day in the Rio Grande Valley. Today's menu is as follows: carne guisada, rice, vegetable delight, and pineapple bits. Never quite figured out what was in that. Anyway, please come out to the pep rally at 7:45 tomorrow morning. We really need to get behind the football team and show them our support. Maybe they'll win a game. All seniors interested in information about colleges in the Northeast, there will be a regional recruiter on campus today. Have a great day. Thank you.

Teacher enters.

TEACHER: Good morning, class. I'm sorry I'm running a little late, I had to e-mail a quiz to a student who's not feeling well today. Is everyone here? Someone please wake up Raúl. Leila, could you . . .

RAÚL: I'm not sleeping.

TEACHER: Good. I'm glad you're with us. Yesterday we had to stop our poetry readings because of a fire drill. Let's finish the poems today and then take the quiz over (*insert title of a piece of literature*). Leila, I think you were next.

LEILA: Sir, I finished my poem right when the fire drill started. Raúl's next.

RAÚL: Shut up, Leila!

LEILA: You shut up.

TEACHER: Leila, please try and calm down.

LEILA: Me? What about him?

Raúl looks at Leila and smirks because she got in trouble.

TEACHER: Raúl? Are you ready to read?

Raúl doesn't reply. He slowly gets up and goes to the front of the room. He pulls out a roll of toilet paper on which his poem is written. Begins reading his poem.

RAÚL: Corporate Caca. (*Milagros and Leila are shocked by Raúl's poem.*)

Shoving your theology down my throat at a million bytes per second.

You're in good hands . . .

Our elected leaders sporting Nike shoes between exfoliations and law alterations.

Lies. It's what's for dinner.

Holding the cure to all known diseases.

Fading the numbers on their calculators.

Teaching the masses to live beyond their means.

Diamonds are forever . . . because so much is riding on your tires.

Live in your world, play in ours.

Corporate caca.

Wipe!

Raúl goes back to his seat.

TEACHER: Well, that was interesting, Raúl. It's always good for the class to hear their peers' views of the corporate model in this country. One based on capitalism and greed.

MILAGROS: Mr. Flores!

TEACHER: I mean, that's what Raúl's poem was trying to explain, I think. Anyway, let's get ready for the quiz. Everything off your desk except for a pen.

All: Come on, sir!

Lights out. Sound: Gym noises that fade out halfway through scene.

Lights up. Leila and Milagros start in aisle and make their way on stage and have a seat on a bench that is already on stage. They are holding their P.E. clothes, very obviously. We can see their sneakers, shorts, etc. As scene progresses we slowly hear sounds of shoes squeaking on basketball court.

LEILA: Did you understand it?

MILAGROS: What?

LEILA: Raúl's poem.

MILAGROS: *(Obviously thinking about something else.)* Huh?

LEILA: *(Forcefully.)* Raúl's poem. Your head's in the clouds today. *(Pause.)* Well, did you like it?

MILAGROS: Yeah. It was really good.

LEILA: My cousin Debbie told me that Raúl was an artist. That he could paint anything, like the Tasmanian Devil and Cantinflas.

MILAGROS: I've seen him draw in class. He's really talented. He's just a little angry.

Pause.

LEILA: I don't know why we have to take P.E. It's such a waste of time.

MILAGROS: What, you don't like these outfits?

Beat.

MILAGROS: *(We finally begin to see what Milagros has been thinking about.)* Did you hear the announcements?

LEILA: I know, carne guisada. Every Thursday, carne guisada.

MILAGROS: No, the college recruiter.

LEILA: Yeah, what about it?

MILAGROS: I don't know; I was thinking about going to talk to him.

LEILA: In that outfit? *(Pointing at her P.E. clothes.)*

MILAGROS: No, seriously. I think it would be fun to go away to college.

LEILA: Go away from what? Home?

MILAGROS: Well, maybe not forever, but to go see what's out there.

LEILA: You want to know what's out there? (*Milagros reacts, thinking Leila is going to offer some insight into "what's out there."*) People that don't understand us.

MILAGROS: I'll make them understand me. (*Changing the subject.*) Did you see the new stadium?

LEILA: How could I miss it?

MILAGROS: They get everything.

LEILA: New uniforms every season.

MILAGROS: A jumbo tron.

LEILA: It's amazing how much money schools spend on that kind of stuff.

Leila and Milagros become more and more animated.

MILAGROS: What about things for the other students? Not everyone plays sports.

LEILA: They should spend the same amount of money on other stuff, like a movie night or field trips to the beach.

MILAGROS: No, they should start a film program where we could learn how to make movies.

LEILA: Yeah, that would be cool. We could have our own production company!

MILAGROS: Yeah! Chihuahua Productions!

BOTH: (*Making fun of themselves.*) Stooooopid!

LEILA: We could make telenovelas and documentaries about local bands. (*They laugh.*)

Beat.

MILAGROS: You know, I think that's why a lot of students don't finish school. What for? There's no incentive. Athletes can get scholarships and popularity. What do kids who study hard get? They get made fun of.

LEILA: There you go again, Milagros, wanting to save the world.

MILAGROS: Not save the world, Leila, just myself.

Pause.

LEILA: Well let me know what the college recruiter says.

MILAGROS: Really?

LEILA: Hey, you're not the only one who wants to go to college. I want to go too.

MILAGROS: Well, I'll let you know.

Lights out. Bench removed. Musical interlude, which ends with sounds of laughter.

Lights up. Scene begins with laughter (sound cue). Tía Mana voiced over in this scene from offstage. Teacher addresses audience as the class.

TEACHER: That was very good, Gavino. Your hero is your dog. I have to say that's a first. Milagros, you're next. OK, class, let's all pay attention. Our heroes are very important to us.

Milagros goes to the front of the classroom. She begins reading her essay.

MILAGROS: Land owner. Caregiver. A woman of respect in an age where men's only need for women was to get the morning paper. My hero. My tía Mana. A lifelong friend to all who are lucky enough to make her acquaintance. She is more than a century old and boasts not one but two appearances on the *Today* show—well, her picture. She has a parrot named Pájaro who only speaks Spanish. All my life my tía Mana has helped me and my family with anything we have ever needed. Ever since I can remember, Tía Mana has encouraged me to be myself and look for the beauty in life. My tía Mana used to babysit me when I was small. Tía let me crawl anywhere I wanted. My other tías worried that I'd fall down the stairs or get stuck under a bed. But Tía Mana told them . . .

MANA: If my peacocks, ducks, and chickens can walk anywhere they want, so can Milagros. And if little Milagros had wings I would let her fly.

MILAGROS: All my other tías just laughed. She was so funny that way. On my tenth birthday, Tía made me a bright dress and a cake with the same colors. My uncles played "Happy Birthday" on their accordions and everyone sang as I stood in front of my cake. Tía Mana leaned toward me and asked . . .

MANA: What are you going to wish for?

MILAGROS: I don't know. What do you think I should wish for?

MANA: A plane ticket to anywhere you want to go. You should fly far away, mija. To all the places that you've read about.

MILAGROS: I couldn't believe it. She got the tickets for me and my Mom. That was the kind of stuff my tía used to do for me all the time. Things that made me feel important. She is truly an inspiration. I know I must be the luckiest person in the world to have her in my life. So that's my hero, my tía Mana. *(Sounds of clapping.)* Thank you.

Lights out. Sounds of clapping into the bell ringing into principal's announcements.

Lights up. Recruiter walks on stage during announcement. He is lost, looking at a school map trying to get to the library.

Principal pauses throughout scene because of the carne guisada that has not settled in his stomach.

PRINCIPAL: *(Voice-over.)* Can I have your attention. This is your principal speaking. Just a reminder that all seniors interested in talking to the college recruiter, he will be in the library for the remainder of the afternoon. Thank you. Oh . . . one more thing has been brought to my attention. Apparently the carne guisada was not very good and some students have been getting sick. So if you had the carne guisada and aren't feeling well, feel free to come to the nurse's office. Just get a pass from your teacher. Thank you.

Raúl is walking on stage with a backpack. College Recruiter is walking the opposite way, toward Raúl.

RECRUITER: Excuse me, young man, but could you tell me where the library is? I'm the college recruiter. I seem to be lost.

RAÚL: Just keep going down the *uhh! (Raúl grips his stomach in pain.)*

RECRUITER: Are you OK?

RAÚL: I think it's the carne guisada.

RECRUITER: The what? (*Not familiar with the local dish.)*

RAÚL: I'm gonna puke! (*Raúl runs off stage, making loud puking noises.*

College Recruiter walks off stage confused. The puking noises continue for a few moments after the exchange is over.

Milagros and Leila enter. Milagros is nervous throughout scene because she will soon talk to the College Recruiter.

LEILA: What are you doing after school?

MILAGROS: I'm going to Tía Mana's.

LEILA: What for?

MILAGROS: Oh, just to say hi. I haven't seen her all week; she's been busy.

LEILA: That woman is so active. I hope I have her energy when I reach her age.

MILAGROS: I just hope I reach her age.

LEILA: So, are you gonna talk to the recruiter?

MILAGROS: Yeah, I'm fixing to go right now. I'm just nervous.

RAÚL: (*Enters, wiping off his mouth.)* You're wasting your time.

LEILA: *(Ready to fight and defend her friend, Valley style.)* Shut up, Raúl. What do you know?

RAÚL: I know enough not to ever want to go to a place that corrupts the mind.

MILAGROS: What are you talking about?

RAÚL: Colleges weren't made for us. They were invented for the privileged. For the rich. Just look at the test to get in them. Standardized testing. Or if you don't know what some fancy word like "reticent" means, you can't go to their schools.

LEILA: Reti— what?

RAÚL: We don't belong there. We belong in the fields where they want us. That's why we were built close to the ground. To pick the pretty flowers that go on their tables.

LEILA: You've been sniffing some of that paint.

RAÚL: You don't have to accept it. You can play along and pretend that it's not true.

MILAGROS: You're smart; you can go to college.

RAÚL: I am smart; that's why I'm not going to college. Why go to college?

MILAGROS: To get an education.

RAÚL: And then what?

MILAGROS: . . . Well, get a job.

RAÚL: I can get a job and make more money at [*insert the name of a local grocery store*] than most people make right out of college *and* get benefits. So why would I want to throw away good money on an education when I'm going to have to get a job when I get out anyway?

LEILA: *(Completely missing the point.)* I didn't know that [*insert the name of a local grocery store*] paid so well.

MILAGROS: Leila, stop. It's about pride, Raúl. How many people from the Valley go to college and come back and make a difference in their communities? We need to control our history. You don't think that's important?!

RAÚL: *(Backing off.)* Why you trippin', girl?

MILAGROS: *(Really feeling her own power.)* It's not important if you go to some university you can't pronounce; it's just important that you go.

LEILA: You're right, Milagros.

RAÚL: You'll never see me in any of those prisons.

Pause.

LEILA: What's that?

MILAGROS: What?

LEILA: You smell it?

MILAGROS: What?

LEILA: It smells like vomit.

RAÚL: I don't smell anything . . .

LEILA: It's Raúl!

They both make sniffing sounds and slowly look at Raúl.

RAÚL: What? I didn't do it. (*Raúl, embarrassed, runs off. Girls laugh.*)

Lights down. Transition music.

Set: a desk and a chair. Lights up. Milagros nervously walks in.

MILAGROS: Excuse me, are you the college recruiter?

RECRUITER: Have a seat. What's your name?

MILAGROS: Milagros Valdez.

RECRUITER: Let me see (*Begins looking in his files for her information.*)

MILAGROS: What is yours?

RECRUITER: (*Surprised.*) I'm sorry?

MILAGROS: Your name. You know mine.

RECRUITER: Of course. Charles. Charles Macintyre.

MILAGROS: Where are you from?

RECRUITER: Boston, well, originally from Brighton. It's right outside the city.

MILAGROS: The meatpacking part of town.

RECRUITER: Yeah . . . how did you know?

MILAGROS: It's amazing what you can learn at the library.

RECRUITER: Amazing. Milagros, *(Recruiter pronounces her name "Milly-gross" throughout scene)* right? That's an interesting name. What does it mean?

MILAGROS: Miracles.

RECRUITER: Really?

MILAGROS: My tía Mana, Aunt Mana, named me that because my mother was forty-five years old and wasn't supposed to have any more children. My mother told me that my aunt walked to St. Joan of Arc Catholic Church and lit a vela, a candle, for me every day from the time she learned my mother was pregnant until I was born. So I guess I'm a miracle.

RECRUITER: I guess you are. Well, back to the task at hand. So, Milagros, are you interested in attending college?

MILAGROS: Yes, I am. I think it's important for Mexican Americans to go to college so they can come back educated and contribute to their communities.

RECRUITER: That's very progressive.

MILAGROS: I like to think so.

RECRUITER: Well, have you taken the SAT?

MILAGROS: Twice.

RECRUITER: Good. Well, let me pull your file . . . *(Begins looking at her file.)* Very impressive. SAT scores are high, GPA looks good, NHS, student council, and community outreach. Tell me, Milagros, have you considered applying to an out-of-state school?

MILAGROS: You mean, where rich kids go?

RECRUITER: Well, yes, there are wealthy kids who attend those schools, sure. But they do boast a large number of minority students and foreigners.

MILAGROS: I'm no foreigner.

RECRUITER: Of course not. My point is that these schools take the best. No matter what your socioeconomic background may be.

MILAGROS: *(Pause.)* Are you telling me that I can go to Harvard?

RECRUITER: Well, you have to apply first, but I think so.

MILAGROS: Are you telling me Milagros Valdez can go to Princeton?

RECRUITER: Yes!

MILAGROS: Are you telling me this Latina from the Valley can go to Yale?

RECRUITER: Yes! Yes!

MILAGROS: *(Goes down center.)* Tía Mana will be so proud. What will Mom and Dad say? *(Beat.)* Big trees and buildings. Birds singing songs I've never heard. The coast, subways, trains, snow!!! . . . like a dream . . .

RECRUITER: Milagros!

MILAGROS: Yes! *(Realizing she's been talking to herself.)* Oh, I'm sorry! *(Trying to calm down.)*

RECRUITER: It's quite all right.

MILAGROS: It's like a dream, Mr. Macintyre.

RECRUITER: For a boy from the meatpacking part of town, it was for me too.

MILAGROS: Well, how much would it cost?

RECRUITER: Including meals, books, and housing . . . about $35,000 a year. *(Sound cue of a train begins.)*

Milagros's jaw drops; she's crushed and slowly walks off stage as if she's just been hit by a train.

RECRUITER: Milagros, wait! I haven't talked to you about scholarships or financial aid! Wait! Milagros, wait!

Lights fade. Somber music continues and ends with phone ringing.

Dim lights up. We see Milagros walking on stage in the same way she left the last scene. She is looking around, searching, trying to recover from the whirlwind in the

library. She is in this state of mind for about half a minute until she finally screams. Remaining lights up.

MILAGROS: "TÍA MANA!" *(Music stops at same time as line.)*

Sound cue: phone rings. Mana walks on stage with a phone in hand.

MANA: Hola, mija. Why are you calling me? You're supposed to be in school.

MILAGROS: I'm still in school, Tía.

MANA: Good, school is important. Don't forget that. I know you're a senior and you want to spend time with your friends, but . . .

MILAGROS: No, Tía, I just wanted to call and tell you hi.

MANA: Well . . .

MILAGROS: Well, what?

MANA: Well, tell me hi.

MILAGROS: Hi.

MANA: OK, gotta go. Pájaro needs to be fed. *(Sound cue: Pájaro squawks.)*

MILAGROS: No, no, don't go, Tía.

MANA: What is it, Milagros? I know you too well. Are you going to tell me or am I going to have to walk over to your school and get it from you?

MILAGROS: *(Frazzled.)* OK, OK. I talked to this recruiter from college and we talked about snow and it's gonna cost too much money, I don't know what to do and he said he thought I could go but I don't know, I just left him there and then I called you!

MANA: Milagros, you're not making any sense. Now slow down and tell me what happened.

MILAGROS: The college recruiter said I could go to a big university.

MANA: Well, I knew that. You've studied very hard, mija.

MILAGROS: But then he told me how much it was going to cost.

MANA: Milagros, I have always told you that I will help you with college.

MILAGROS: I know, but I just don't know what to do. It's just so much money.

MANA: Follow your dreams, Milagros.

Milagros is beginning to relax but still nervous about her parents.

MILAGROS: My dreams seem to be very expensive, Tía.

MANA: Mija, fly as far as your wings will take you.

MILAGROS: I'm worried about what Dad is going to say.

MANA: Let me deal with him. You just relax and get back to class!

MILAGROS: OK, Tía . . .

Milagros remains on stage for a moment contemplating. She is feeling confident again. Lights down. Transition music.

10

Milagros's home. Kitchen table and chairs. After school. Milagros is a little tentative; she's about to drop some bombs about her future. Lights up.

MOM: Hey, mija, how was your day? Mine was terrible. The air condition broke at work, all the ladies in the office were all sweaty, and we were so busy.

MILAGROS: That's awful, Mom.

MOM: Whatever you do, mija, please go to college and get a good job so you won't have to work hard like me.

MILAGROS: Well, that's what I kinda want to talk to you about. I have some good news, Mom.

MOM: What is it?

MILAGROS: I talked to a college recruiter today and he said that I have a good chance to go to an out-of-state school.

MOM: Oh, mija, I'm so proud of you. You really deserve it, Milagros.

They embrace and share a sweet moment. Dad walks in.

DAD: What's going on? Are you sick? Why are you crying? ¿Qué te pasó?

MOM: *(Helping Milagros wipe her tears.)* No, she's fine, David. She just had a good day at school.

DAD: I don't understand you females. When I have a good day you never see me crying.

MOM: I've never seen you cry. Well, except that time the [*insert name of local sports team*] lost.

DAD: Don't bring that up. You know that's still a very sensitive subject. So, what happened today, Milagros?

MILAGROS: I talked to a college recruiter . . .

DAD: Good.

MILAGROS: And he said I had an opportunity . . .

DAD: Of course, you have many opportunities.

MILAGROS: To go away to college.

DAD: Away?!! Away where? There are plenty of colleges here in Texas, Milagros.

MILAGROS: I know, but how many people from the Valley get this chance?

DAD: Who's going to pay for this? You know we can't afford that, Milagros. We're barely making ends meet.

MOM: He's right, Milagros, we can't afford it.

MILAGROS: *(Hurt that her mom changed her opinion.)* MOM! . . . Well, Tía Mana said she would help me.

DAD: She can't help you. She needs that money for the nursing home.

MILAGROS: What nursing home? You can't put Tía in a nursing home!

DAD: Well, who's going to take care of her? If you're far away at school, you can't do it, and your mother and me have jobs.

MILAGROS: But there's nothing wrong with her. She's never even been sick. She does everything herself.

MOM: Sí, pero she's like a thousand years old and she's been on the *Today* show a hundred times. You think she's going to live forever?

MILAGROS: She has the tías. They'll take care of her.

DAD: They can't even take care of themselves. They're in their eighties. Look, Milagros, it's up to you if you want to go, but if you're going to leave your home, the place where you grew up, the only place in this world where people love you, don't be surprised to come home and find all your tías in a nursing home.

MOM: David!

Milagros runs off stage whimpering. She can't believe that her dad just did that.

Lights out. Stage: remove kitchen table and place chairs for Tía Mana's house. Three chairs are on stage. No music.

Lights up.

MILAGROS: All night I imagined my tía in a nursing home and Pájaro in a cage with no one to talk to, all because I wanted to go to some distant college where it snowed in the winter. I couldn't stop worrying. That afternoon I sat outside the balcony with my tía. I watched Tía, looking for any signs that she was slowing down.

Lights down.

Raúl's music begins. Raúl is tagging a wall when the scene begins. Lights up. Raúl's present canvas is a brick wall with the beginnings of his latest work, a painting of his abuelo.

RAÚL: Tagging. Your name adorns the walls, the doors, the buses, the libraries, bathrooms, billboards, every telephone booth, every school, every court. Spreading your identity to the eyes of a thousand viewers. Innocent bystanders. That will carve into their minds the image which you have created. They will know that you are out there. That you exist. And that you resist. *(Recruiter walks in and sees Raúl painting.)* Turning their sanctuaries, their clean slates into canvases for you to desecrate. Inflicting their innocence with so much fervor, so much shock. And then you got them right by their spirit. Holding it in your hand. Caressing it.

Recruiter accidentally drops his briefcase. Raúl is startled.

RECRUITER: I'm sorry. *(Recruiter picks up the briefcase.)*

RAÚL: *(Aggressively.)* You need something?

RECRUITER: Do I need something? No.

RAÚL: You a cop?

RECRUITER: No.

RAÚL: Well, what do you want? Can't you see I'm busy?

RECRUITER: Is this your art?

RAÚL: Yeah, what of it?

RECRUITER: Very impressive.

RAÚL: What are you, a critic?

RECRUITER: I know a few.

RAÚL: Look, I would love to chitchat about . . . whatever it is you people like to chitchat about, but I don't like to leave my work unfinished.

RECRUITER: That's what I want to talk to you about.

RAÚL: What?

RECRUITER: Your art. It's really good.

RAÚL: You want to play games? there's a Halo Reach game in the bakery around the corner.

RECRUITER: I'm serious.

RAÚL: So am I. You need change?

RECRUITER: Look, I'd like to help. I represent colleges in the Northeast.

RAÚL: And I represent the south side, vato. What's your point?

RECRUITER: My point is that you have talent. (*Beat.*) No one's ever told you that before, have they? Why don't you tell me about your art?

RAÚL: This is my abuelo. He died. This is him. I have his eyes and the lines in his face will be my lines years from now.

RECRUITER: (*Beat.*) Have you ever thought about art school?

RAÚL: Like college?

RECRUITER: Well sort of; it's a conservatory, a place where you can continue doing your art.

RAÚL: They have those? (*Recruiter nods.*) Hey, you're that college recruiter guy . . .

RECRUITER: Yes . . . that's my job. Match up schools with the best students.

RAÚL: The best? You're in the wrong neighborhood, Yankee Doodle. I'm not even in the top 30 percent.

RECRUITER: That's just a number. There's also talent, which tests can't measure. You have a portfolio?

RAÚL: A what?

RECRUITER: A portfolio, you know, a collection of your work.

RAÚL: I have a few pictures that I took with my little sister's camera.

RECRUITER: You do? That's great. Tell you what. I'll give you the addresses of some art schools you can send your photos to, and see what they say.

RAÚL: But hey, aren't those schools expensive?

RECRUITER: Of course, but those schools want the best and they're willing to pay for it. If you're serious about your art.

RAÚL: I take my work very seriously.

RECRUITER: Well, then, I'll give you the info.

RAÚL: Órale, sir! (*Beat.*) Art school.

Lights fade. Quick sound byte to finish scene, then crickets to set up Tía Mana's. Get bench on stage.

Milagros and Mana are seated. Lights up on Milagros and Mana sitting on her balcony.

MILAGROS: *(Trying to be discreet.)* How are you feeling today, Tía Mana?

MANA: Every day is another day. *(Beat.)* Mijita, I have known you all your life, and I know when you are troubled. Bueno, dime. What's wrong?

MILAGROS: Ay, Tía. It's just that Mom and Dad said I shouldn't go far away to college. They think I should stay here and take care of you.

MANA: *(Laughing.)* Take care of me? I can take care of myself.

MILAGROS: Si, Tía, but they say you are getting old, y que . . . *(Trying to find the word.)*

MANA: Estoy vieja. *(Laughs.)* Mira, I can take care of myself. I always have. They don't want you to go away because they never went anywhere.

MILAGROS: But if you do get to a point where you can't take care of yourself, they'll put you in a nursing home. Y Tía, I would feel terrible if that happened. And what would happen to Pájaro?

Sound of a diesel truck. Sound of the truck door closing. Mana pauses.

MANA: Is that your father's truck?

MILAGROS: *(Nods.)*

Dad joins them.

DAD: Hola, Tía. *(Tries to give her a kiss.)*

MANA: *(Doesn't let him get close.)* Sit down, please . . . Ándale!

Beat.

MANA: How are you?

DAD: Good. *(Pause.)* How are you, Tía?

MANA: Not good. *(Sarcastically.)* I'm getting so old!

Dad looks at Milagros.

MANA: Doesn't Pájaro have pretty feathers?

DAD: Oh, yes, beautiful feathers. (*Milagros is surprised; she's never heard her dad talk like that.*)

MANA: ¿Y sabes qué? Pájaro can fly. Pero I always tie a string around his ankle because I'm afraid of him flying away and never coming back. But if you have beautiful wings, you were meant to fly, no?

Dad keeps silent.

MANA: Diosito gives everyone gifts, and it's a sin not to use them. Y tambien, it's a sin not to let people use the gifts Diosito blessed them with.

Dad looks at Mana and she looks at him, waiting for a response.

DAD: Si, Tía, it's a sin.

MANA: I love Pájaro more than most anything else. The bird has brought me so much happiness. I've had him for more than seventy years, and he knows all about our family. He watched you get married and has seen the birth of all your kids. Sí, I love this bird, pero I have kept him in a cage all this time. Eso no es amor. No, love does not cage. Love sets free. I love only one person more than I love this bird. I love Milagros, pero I want her to be happy. To be free. Mija, open Pájaro's cage. (*Beat.*) Go ahead, mija, open it.

Mana and Dad freeze as Milagros describes what happens.

MILAGROS: I opened the cage door wide, and Pájaro blinked at me, confused. I reached in and took off his ankle bracelet and stepped back. Pájaro jumped from his mesquite branch to the edge of the birdcage and fluttered his wings. My dad stood up. I could hear him saying, "Close the door," but he sounded far away. My tía looked blissful. Pájaro squawked and said, "Milagros, qué bonita," and started to sing. He flew toward me, and I could feel the brush of feathers—hundreds and hundreds of feathers of parakeets singing, and Tía Mana on the tips of her toes throwing her arms up, calling to us, *(Sound cue of birds flapping, building . . .)*

MANA: Fly, fly, fly!!!

Milagros and her tía join hands, looking up to the sky, happy. The College Recruiter enters.

RECRUITER: Hello. Hello. Am I interrupting anything?

MILAGROS: Mr. Macintyre? That's the man I told you about.

RECRUITER: Hello, Milagros. *Milagros walks over and shakes his hand.*

MILAGROS: What are you doing here? I thought you'd be on an airplane by now.

RECRUITER: Well, actually I am running a little bit late, but I wanted to come by and give you some good news.

MILAGROS: Well, this is my father and my tía Mana.

RECRUITER: Very nice to meet you, Mr. Valdez, and very nice to meet you too, ma'am. You must be very proud of Milagros. I have to tell you that I was very impressed when I met her today. I was so impressed that I called the dean of admissions at MIT. I informed them of Milagros's grades and hard work . . . and they would like to offer Milagros a substantial scholarship.

MILAGROS: Really? *(Excited, then quickly withdraws emotion and looks at her tía Mana for strength and then slowly turns to her Dad and says)* Dad?

A heavy moment passes. Dad looks at his daughter. And then turns his attention to the Recruiter.

DAD: Not so fast, Mr. MIT. Not until we talk to Harvard first. *(Dad is beaming.)*

Milagros, Tía Mana, and Dad all hug, then they reach out and hug the Recruiter. All is well. Lights down. Epilogue music.

14

BUS DRIVER: Well, it's the end of the road. A road far traveled yet you never left your seat. Your caboose stayed in one place. Immovable objects. Like Stonehenge. Glued to the cushions like paint. Yes, my people, we, us, nosotros, my homegirls and boys. My peeps. (*Beat.*) So you finished this journey. It's complete for the moment, but life goes on whether you get on the bus or not. Whether you're willing to play the game or not. Yes, a game. Of biblical proportions. Come get your portion, vato! What are you waiting for? An invitation? You got yours. You were born into this crazy beautiful world. It's up to you. (*Beat.*) So what happened? Eh? To Milagros, Leila, Raúl. Milagros, Leila, Raúl, oh my! Well, Raúl's going to art school in Boston, thinking he's a big deal. He's painting pictures of the Rio Grande Valley for those Yankees. Leila? She's working really hard. I saw her the other day. She works at [*insert name of a local grocery store*] during the day and goes to college at night so she can become a nurse. Y Milagros, well what can I say, the homegirl did it, she's at MIT showing those people up there what's up. And Tía Mana, she was on the *Today* show for the third time, qué bonita. And me, well I'm still driving this bus . . . Now I only have one thing to say to you before this show is over . . . Get off my bus, AND GET BACK TO CLASS!

Lights out. Epilogue music ends. Pause. Curtain music begins.

Lights up. Curtain call. Actors take their bows.

Lights out, curtain music fades, house lights up, pre/post show music begins.